The Three Investigators

Mystery
of the
Ghost
Train

Text By Hector Sebastian

Based on Characters created by
Robert Arthur

Cover Art by T K Kwiatuowski

Collins   William Collins and Sons, Publishers

The original cover of this book came about when a fan, Daniel Storm, contacted one of the original book cover artists.

He commissioned Robert Adragna to come up with a concept cover given only the known (missing) title. Because I could not get permission to use *that* art (which was perfect!) I found the background for this new cover on a website filled with free-to-use artwork that was attributed to artist T K Kwiatuowski ... I thank them both!

Contents

Hector Sebastian Makes an Introduction

Hello, once again, young friends! I am delighted to have to opportunity to introduce this exciting adventure... and saddened at the same time.

You see, this will be the final accounting of our Three Investigators in which I shall play any part. It has been a wonderful journey getting to know Jupiter, Pete and Bob, and to be given the honor of these introductions once their original mentor, the great movie director, Alfred Hitchcock, passed from this firmament.

I must tell you that this mystery adventure nearly never was recorded when Bob Andrews, known often as Records and the chronicler of these stories, lost his notes. Or, rather, he misplaced them, and then discovered that his mother, in a fit of unbridled housekeeping, had simply picked up and discarded a stack of papers she termed, "meaningless scribblings." He was, to say the very least, despondent over their loss until his two colleagues, Jupe and Pete, decided to help him recreate them.

I must proudly tell you that I assisted them in some great way by using my word processor to help capture everything they discussed when attempting to recreate everything they had done.

What you will soon be reading is a tale involving a cross-country trip on what was advertised as being a "ghost-haunted train journey to rattle your bones and cause gooseflesh to race up and down the spines of even the most hardened travelers." That is marketing speak for "We are going to try to make you believe that the normal shaking and squeakings and bumps of an old train are being cause by the 'spirits.'"

Oh, what fun they had until it all appeared to become too

real! Then, the game began and they put all their mental and physical strengths to work to solve an apparent murder of someone who was supposedly never on the train!

And then another death of... ah, but that would be telling too much! Mustn't give away the story, huh?

I am racing ahead and ought not to spoil any of the fun. Oh, and in case you are wondering why my name appears on the cover page of the book, it is because I have taken financial responsibility for the monies earned by the boys for sales of this book, and no publisher would let fourteen-year-olds have that honor or responsibility. Believe me, as each check appears in the post I go to the bank and deposit it in their three identical accounts. Happily, they now have most of their college educations paid for.

All I must say in conclusion is that these past couple of years have been among my most treasured in my fifty-some-odd years on this Earth.

Thank you for reading the ramblings of an old author.

Hector Sebastian

1

"A Vacation Seems to be Appropriate"

"DO YOU realize that with our solving that mystery of the collector with an attitude problem, we've come close to fifty cases and all but one small one solved?" The question came from Jupiter Jones, three months shy of turning fifteen and what most adults would call fat, or at least chubby, but he preferred to think of his body type as stocky. It was directed to his two best friend, Bob Andrews and Pete Crenshaw as they sat inside an old mobile home trailer that was deeply buried under several tons of what could kindly be termed "junk."

The trailer was their Headquarters and it was the center of their investigative business, The Three Investigators. It had been since they turned twelve and started to solve local mysteries the police just didn't want to bother with. Things such as the mysterious disappearance of a neighbor's cat from inside a locked house and a secured cage.

It had been easy to them. Jupe—Jupiter's more commonly used name—had spotted that family's housekeeper five days earlier as she came by one afternoon. She left the front door wide open and even took the caged animal out onto the front porch while she dusted and vacuumed.

Not being a particularly stupid cat, Jupe deduced it had simply used a paw to lift the latch and had slipped out and away. Then, the trio staked out the local city dump where a lot of cats and some other animals such as skunks and raccoons congregated. Sure enough, within hours the cat, a male curiously named Tinkerbell, sauntered through a hole in the fencing and walked over to a group of other cats who where dining on something that probably was a real treat for them but Jupe thought must be disgusting.

Bob stood up and grabbed the pole onto which they had fashioned a loop of soft rope and headed slowly toward the gathering.

When Tinkerbell turned his head and spotted the lankly youth he scooted swiftly back to the fence and managed to meet one of the other locals face to face. That local, a sleek black animal with a white stripe down its back, turned around and lifted its tail.

The smell hit all three boys' noses in seconds sending them running the opposite direction.

Once they got home and changed out of their smelly clothes, they walked to the neighbor's house to report the sighting—and the dousing—only to find the smell had preceded them. The wife opened the door to their knocks with a big smile and a strained look on her face.

"We came to tell you your cat was at the dump and got hit by a skunk," Jupe began and then realized that Tinkerbell must have come running home for safety, so he finished with, "but as you can tell, or smell, he hightailed it for home. My Aunt Mathilda says that tomato juice liberally spread over the animal and left on for five minutes gets a lot of the stink out."

Mrs Abernathy was thrilled that the family cat was home and also that her teenage daughter was on restrictions for disobeying her parents and so she was the one currently washing the cat.

"You know, I don't think he would have come home if you boys hadn't been there and so I owe you a reward. Let me get my purse."

Her young son came out of a back room laughing and shouting, "Stinkerbell, Stinkerbell!"

From the next room his mother yelled, "Knock that off!"

She returned and handed them each a two-dollar bill before thanking them again and closing the front door.

"All in a days work," Jupe stated to the closed door, "and I think we should use some of this money to buy a big can of tomato juice and get our clothes de-stunk before any adults get wind of them!"

Jupe was the acknowledged leader of the trio. He had a mind that remembered almost everything, had a way with adults who seemed slightly intimidated by the boy who spoke to them as if he were either their equal or possibly a little superior to them. A lot of that self-assurance had come from being a child actor who, at the age of two could remember his lines and recite them better than most adults he worked with. Baby Fatso had been his name back them, or more properly it had been the name of his famous character.

But, back to the mobile home trailer. Jupe's Aunt and Uncle owned a junkyard specialising in finding items that could be cleaned or fixed a little and resold that most other such places simply tossed into piles. Officially it was known as Jones Salvage Yard.

His Uncle had purchased the trailer when Jupe was about eleven and had parked it in a remote part of the yard intending to repair it, "some day..." but Jupe had seized on the idea that it might be better suited as a place he and his friends could hang out in, and so he and the other two picked up the front hitch area from the stump on which it rested one evening, wheeled it back into a recess between a couple piles of other items, and then spent hours covering it up.

It had soon been forgotten and was quickly turned into a secret place for the boys including several possible entrances, all hidden and known mostly to the three.

"I think you'll find we have barely topped forty-seven," Bob said. And, as the one who did all of their records keeping, he would know. "We've done the big forty three plus the first cat things, and then those three small jobs that never went anywhere. So, call it forty-seven."

Jupe appeared to be deep in thought. Finally he came out of it and looked at the others. "Then, it is either time to get that forty eighth mystery or..." and he now looked quite pleased with himself. "Since it is well past spring vacation, and that spanned a whopping two weeks during which we did nothing, we should take a vacation. We've earned it!"

Bob, who had been smiling, was also the Treasurer for their "business" and well knew the state of their bank account. "I hate to be the bearer of discouraging news, but the two of you do realize we have less than one hundred dollars in our account, right?"

Pete's smile also disappeared, but Jupiter kept beaming.

"What?" Bob and Pete asked simultaneously.

"Well, do the two of you recall our experiences with the Ragnarson family and their Viking family gathering? The one where we helped solve the case of that ghost captain and also that bad seed son, Sam Ragnarson?" When his two counterparts nodded, Jupe went on. "Well, you may also recall that I told our Principal, Mr Karl Ragnarson, that we couldn't accept payment." This time there were two very sad nods.

"Okay. Well, both he and his brother, the dentist, decided we ought to be rewarded with more than that grotesque mask he gave us. So, they worked with a cousin, a lawyer in San Bernardino, and found a loophole in California state law dealing with payments to minors. It seems that since our business is not registered or licensed, it is classified as a *hobby* and there are no laws against paying teens for performing their hobbies."

"So..." Bob asked in an awed whisper.

"So, the entire family got together and decided that ten percent of what they all received from the sale of those gold coins they recovered ought to be given to us. Every one of them save for good old Sam figured they'd never have even known about them much less found them if it weren't for The Three Investigators. And so... it is my happy honor to tell you that as of noon today our account has an extra sixteen thousand dollars in it. I figure that if we each take four thousand for our college funds that still leaves us with four thousand and one hundred for the business."

It took the others a few moments to come to grips with the meaning of this, but as it dawned on them, smiles replaced frowns and soon they were whooping and hollering their glee.

"Does that mean we can really go on a vacation?"

Jupiter Jones nodded as solemnly as he possibly could.

"It, indeed, means just that. With school out for the summer in three weeks I know Aunt Mathilda will have a long list of jobs for me, but if we work hard during June my guess is we can take off in July and have a grand time somewhere."

Bob turned to Pete saying, "You know something? I've long thought a vacation is appropriate for us to celebrate being in the detective business now for more than three full years."

"I agree. Jupe? What do you say?"

"I say that we need to go down to the Travel Agency on Via de Las Pas and pick out some brochures to look through."

"I second that," said Bob, the Second Investigator and their Records man.

"Unanimous," proclaimed Pete.

The boys left the Headquarters trailer three minutes later heading out one of the three main entrances to the trailer. This one emptied into an area hidden from view by all who did not know it existed and let them slip out of the junkyard with their bicycles.

Together they pedaled down the frontage road running by the yard heading for the downtown area of Rocky Beach.

They had to wait twenty minutes for the agency people to come back from their lunch. Bob suggested they go have a hamburger someplace but Jupiter was positively bursting to get inside the very second they reopened. When a woman unlocked the front door he was standing so close behind her that she stepped back and her high heel crushed down on his left foot.

He yelped which startled her so much she stepped back with the other heel bringing it squarely down on his right foot.

Jupiter had to sit down on a bench outside the travel agency to recover. By the time he felt he could walk again, five customers had passed them and gone inside.

It annoyed him to the point he had to pause and count to ten during which time another woman passed them and breezed into the agency.

2

The Trio Win Their Passage

IT WAS a busy day at Headquarters looking through the fifteen different brochures they managed to talk the lady at the agency into giving them

"Normally children must bring in an adult," she began telling them until Jupiter interrupted her. He hated it when adults called him or Bob and Pete "children."

"But I'm certain that if your manager knew you were turning away customers with nearly four thousand dollars to spend on a vacation, he might suggest that policy is incorrect." He smiled innocently at her and refused to blink his eyes until she had to turn away feeling very uncomfortable.

She looked back at him after twenty seconds, eyes now narrowed, but his unflagging stare and ingratiating smile got to her again and she simply looked down at her desk and pointed to the rack across the office.

"Over there. Rail journeys, ocean liners, Hawaiian vacations and even bus tours of just about any place on this Earth. Just let me see what you are taking, please."

Not wanting her to feel angry once they left, Jupe showed her the ones they had selected and asked if she would like to have them returned in a day or two.

"We'll be very careful of them, ma'am," he said in his contrite voice. It was one of ten or so tones he managed to use when speaking with adults, all of which came from his brief stint as a child actor.

She waved them toward the door. "No need. No need for

you to come back until you really want to book something."

"A lot of these look like fun," Pete said as they perused a number of the open books and pamphlets back at Headquarters, "but some look downright boring. 'All the wonderful old masters in just eleven countries over fourteen days,' Gee, sound like you'd spend about twenty hours a day on a bus or something!"

Jupiter nodded. "Yes. I've been thinking that for our first ever no parents vacation we ought to be looking at things closer to home. Some place we can't get too far afield from or away from help if we need it. I wonder..." and he began lightly pinching his lower lip, as sure sign he was thinking hard about something.

The other two saw this and became quiet while they waited for him.

Finally he released his lip and said, "Perhaps some sort of resort where you pay one price and you get everything like food and entertainment in the one fee. Then, you remain on that property for the entire stay and I really can't see any of our parents objecting to that. I mean, we'd practically be watched over the entire time!"

But after some reflection even the optimistic Jupiter Jones had to admit it would be a very hard sell for all their parents, or in his case, his Aunt and Uncle who had guardianship of him.

He was right, or partly so.

Bob's parents said they would need to think about it but at least they wanted to know exactly where and when this unaccompanied trip would be.

Pete's father, the more trusting of his parents, was mostly for the idea while his mother was appalled at the thought her little baby might be caught all alone in the big, bad world. Then Mr Creshaw reminded her that their son had been kidnapped, knocked unconscious and beaten up several time with no lasting ill effects. "Besides," he told her, "that was when he and the other two were looking into trouble. This is a vacation, for crying out loud!"

Jupiter had the hardest time. Even though he was technically an emancipated youth, something his parents had arranged in case of their demise, he was the ward of his relatives. Aunt Mathilda had never come to grips with the work he and Bob and Pete did preferring to let herself believe is was nothing more than harmless solving of puzzles and riddles they found in newspapers at the Library.

Uncle Titus knew better but his wife was a powerhouse and could make everyone's lives miserable if she felt she was being ignored or crossed. So, he smiled and shrugged at Jupe as if to say, "If it were up to me... but it isn't!"

Jupe had hoped to hold onto this one, but he blurted out, "I'll give you the entire month of June, once school gets out on the fifth, of five-days-a-week working in the junkyard at least five hours a day if you agree to let me go for a couple weeks in July. I'll tell you exactly where we'll be once we decide on it and even promise to call you every night if I can get to a phone."

Aunt Mathilda knew she was a beaten woman but wanted to make certain Jupiter was deadly serious about doing his chores.

"Absolutely, and cross my heart!" he declared doing just that.

The next morning Bob and Pete reported their varying degrees of success but no outright agreements. Jupe didn't want them to feel badly so he didn't mention that he and his aunt and uncle had come to an agreement the previous evening at 10:15. He was pleased with himself at having outlasted the two adults both used to being asleep no later than 9:00.

What he did report to them was that he had entered them in a contest.

One of the larger, more powerful radio stations in the greater Los Angeles area had been given a set of tickets for a give-away contest. Nearly three times every hour of the broadcast day, running from six in the morning until eleven at night, a recorded message was played announcing:

"And now, a reminder for all our loyal Kay-Lax listeners, of the contest of the century! Be our lucky winner and receive not one, not two or even three, but four tickets on the Ghost Train, one of the newest adventures available in all of the United States! Just send in a postcard with your name, address and phone number where we might reach you on Friday, the twentieth day of this month at exactly five-o-five in the afternoon. That is just minutes after our super drawing. Please, only one entry per person per day! And gooo-ooo-ooo-ddd luck to everybody-y-y-y-y!!!"

The message went on a few more lines ending with the station's street address and a request that all cards have the words "GHOST TRAIN CONTEST" printed in block letters on the bottom of the card under the station's address.

"Over the past three weeks I've sent a post card in every day, Monday through Saturday. The drawing will be the day after tomorrow. If we win, and there is little hope of it because the odds are so far stacked against us, but *if* we should win it will mean a week or more trip that we don't need to pay for because the train is paid for for up to four people and flights back to Los Angeles from New Orleans are included for the same people!"

He told them how the train follows the route of the Sunset Limited through Arizona, New Mexico, Texas and ending in New Orleans, Louisiana.

"Just over seven days with stopovers in Phoenix, El Paso and Houston. Something like five hours in each to get off and sight see and buy souvenirs."

Pete was a bit of a pessimist and he said, "Fat chance we have. I'll bet a million people sent in hundreds of cards each. We have as much a chance of winning as I have of passing Mrs Zimerlee's Advanced Civics class this term with an A. And that is about zilch!"

"Anything's worth a shot and it only cost the price of a few stamps. I already had the postcard sized paper," Jupe said a little defensively.

They let the matter drop until the afternoon of the drawing. All three crowded around the radio in Headquarters half an hour before the announced time.

"I'm not going to be disappointed," Pete said. He repeated it like a mantra for a minute until Bob told him to "Clam up!"

"Yeah," Jupe added. "Positive thinking is called for. Just like in that *Peter Pan* show they put on TV every other summer. Think lovely thoughts!"

"Hush. I think it's about to happen," Bob stated.

The Headquarters went dead quiet and Jupe was about to fiddle with the radio when the disc jockey came back on.

"Sorry. folks. A bit of one of those old technical problems. But, everything is hunky-dorry and we're about to pull one of the cards all of your real-l-l-lly great listeners sent in, And, not to discourage you, but we received thousands and

17

thousands and thousands of them! And so, after a word from some of our favorite sponsors, we'll get right to it."

This was followed by nearly five minutes of radio spots, advertising jingles and insincere-sounding announcers hawking their products.

"Well, those were just great. This is Marvellous Marvin Marlberg, your Kay-Lax morning man working hard and into the afternoon today and we're all here to find out just who has won our fabulous trip for four on the Ghost Train."

He read from a page they could all hear being rustled that obviously had been written by someone at the train company.

"Okay. The time has come, as the walrus said, ha-ha-ha, to do the drawing. We'll stall no longer. So... the winner of the trip of a lifetime... all courtesy of The Ghost Train Incorporated and KLAX is..." The sound of a wire door being opened was followed by rustling of the many cards they had received. Then, the door snapped shut and the announcer came back on. *"It is a mister Juniper Jones of Rocky Reach. No, wait, that must be a B as in Beach. I'm really not certain where that is but this card says it's some place in California. Congratulations to Juniper!"*

Bob and Pete looked at the First Investigator in time to watch his eye roll upwards and he slumped to the floor.

3
The Disappearing Train

WHEN THE day came, Uncle Titus reluctantly allowed the boys to be driven to the station in Los Angeles by Mr Crenshaw in the large family sedan.

Union Station in the city was a beautiful, old stucco and Spanish tile building. The boys were fascinated to see it was situated close to Dodger Stadium, home field of their favorite baseball team.

Mr Crenshaw drove to the parking lot and found a space close to the doors. All three boys had packed lightly so they took their own suitcases while Pete's dad grabbed a duffel bag his wife had packed with food for the trip, refusing to believe the tickets also included all meals, plus clean underwear for Pete… "Just in case!"

The local television station associated with KLAX radio was going to send a camera crew until they found out it was "just a bunch of kids!" They suddenly announced they had, "Another event to cover." None of the three were sorry about it.

Inside the station, the four of them stood in awe. There were not just the one level inside, there were at least three they could see. On the ground level were about a dozen ticket windows each one doing brisk business. Pete grabbed his father's arm and gave it a tug.

"We need to go trade in our vouchers for real tickets, Dad."

"Actually, son, I don't think that is necessary. Says right here on the back, 'This voucher is to be presented to the train Conductor once this passenger is on board.' We can check at the door to the trains, but I think your three are good to go!"

They all turned to see what had begun making a loud clackity sound and saw that a huge status board, perhaps fifty feet wide and twenty tall, was in the process of changing. As one line disappeared, the line below it was rebuilt in its place from rotating sets of letters and numbers all spinning around to make words and numbers. The process continued until the entire board had been reworked.

Bob, the more studious of the three spotted the listing for their train.

"Says track thirteen," he told them, finding that he had a cold shiver running down his spine. He wasn't particularly superstitious, but…

Mr Crenshaw scanned the various archways along the far wall until he spotted the one listing: **TRACKS 11-16**

The passed though the arch and found themselves in a short line, a man in a blue uniform and box-style cap standing at a podium at the front. He was doing something with a hand stamp and then he made a motion, calling out, "Next!"

He repeated his actions of checking tickets and vouchers before stamping them, pointing to the correct track and the shouting for more customers.

He glanced at the boys' voucher, his brow scrunched.

"Says here you there will be traveling unaccompanied by an adult. Not too sure I like that. What's the story here?"

Jupe stepped forward being the best at speaking to adults.

"Well, sir, I won the radio station KLAX contest giving away four ticket on what is called The Ghost Train. The only thing is, none of our parents can take that much time off, so it is just the three of us. Don't worry, though. We know how to act in situations like this. We promise no adults will ever find it necessary to question us or be cross with us or take exception with our behavior."

The ticket man looked at Jupe and then let out a loud laugh.

"By Harry! You are a real pip, young man. Congratulations. My wife must have sent in fifty postcards. I shall have to tell her I met the actual winners." He picked up his stamp and gave it extra emphasis as he brought it down onto the voucher.

"You three have a wonderful trip, and don't let them scare you with all that ghost and goblin nonsense!"

Mr Crenshaw said goodbye to them at the head of the train which was covered by a large green tarp under which workers were to be heard banging on something. They gave their suitcases and bag to a Porter who checked their voucher, made a note of their room and promised the bags would be in the room within the next twenty minutes.

"Plenty of time. Train takes off at five and it's just gone two right now."

"What do we do until then?" Jupe asked him. "Go sit in our room?"

"No. First off there is a passenger lounge part way down the platform. Go in there and show them your voucher and they'll fix you up with a sandwich and a soda. Then there will be a grand tour of the train starting at three-thirty. That starts off at the far end of the train."

They thanked the man and headed down the platform.

After taking advantage of the food and drinks they headed to the far end of the train fifteen minutes early and found that several dozen people had gotten their ahead of them.

When the tour time came, a side door of the car right behind the locomotive opened and a thin man in his twenties dropped to the platform.

"Welcome to the Ghost Train running between Los Angeles, California and New Orleans, Louisiana… if we get that far, that is—" he said in a voice that tried, but failed, to be menacing. The rather bored young man began describing the various parts of the train.

"This locomotive you see before you is one of two, one at each end. We have this Fairbanks-Morse 1946 FM Erie-Built model locomotive running on diesel which powers eight solid steel wheels with its massive 2,000 horse power engine. It is one of about a hundred built and is only one of seven still operating on a regular basis.

"At the back of the train we'll see the other engine which was once used in the far-off land of Mongolia!" He tried to make it sound as if this were a very eerie thing but failed and Jupe noticed many people around him covering their mouths and grins.

The young man continued. "In between are a total of fifteen cars. Only *thirteen* of them will be where you are allowed. The one behind the front engine is the supplies and power management equipment. Dangerous stuff so we keep you out of there for your safety. Don't even try to get in; the door is marked with a big red X and it says 'Do Not Enter!' so just sort of keep away, huh?"

"How can we get forward to tour the engine," a man dressed in a track-style running outfit called out.

"Uhh," the young man obviously had a set speech and the interruption put him off. Finally he said, "No tours. Unless," and he let out a little barking laugh, "you want to climb outside to the roof and walk over the no entry car!"

He tried to laugh but stopped when he saw nobody else was going to join in.

Next, he told then they would be going into the first public car where he would show them a typical room, explain the toilet system in the private bathrooms, walk them through the coupling between cars, along with how to safely move up and down the train, and then take them back out and all the way to the end of the train.

With nearly a hundred and sixty people to go through and the corridors being narrow, he was only able to describe things to groups of ten to twelve at a time.

The boys were in the third group and about the only thing that caught their attention were the bunks.

Every room, except for the one car with the four "Elite" compartments, had four of these bunks about six feet long and just eighteen inches wide. One was also the sofa for the room, and was part of the storage for suitcases and such, there were two seats at the windows that could be turned into a bed, and the other two were hinged nearly five feet above the floor and could be let down on chains when needed. Access to these was via narrow indentations in the walls to be used like ladder steps.

"I wonder what else he wants to show us," Pete pondered aloud as they stood with the first two groups. It took another fifteen minutes to get everyone outside and for their guide to get ahead of the group. More than a few had begun drifting off minutes earlier and he had to shout to them to come back.

He finally got the group together and simply made a "let's go!" motion with his arm before walking to the back of the train.

"This last car before the rear engine is also partially off limits because it is the crew quarters and our private dining facility. But, on days two and three you can sign up with the Chief Conductor, Mr Donlevy who we'll meet in a little bit, and you can take a tour of the rear engine. It's a doozy, I tell you, and has quite a history. Came over here from Mongolia and China on a liner about ten years ago. Nobody knows who put it on and nobody came to claim it.

"What they did find were three skeletons back in the engine

room. Of course, those got taken away so you won't get to see them, but some say..." he paused and tried to get the eerie tone back in his voice, "...some say their ghosts haunt the train as they try to find the fiend that killed them!"

Jupe sighed heavily enough that a dozen adults around him looked at him. They knew what he was thinking and also believe this part of the spiel to be so much flummery.

Not deterred by mutterings from this small group, their guide continued.

"I've seen the ghost of the killer myself," he said boastfully. "All dressed in dark clothes with a black cape and hat pulled down tight over his eyes so you can't see nothing but his nose and mouth! It's real spooky I tell you."

"Have you seen an actual ghost?" came a question from the back of the group.

"Well, of course. Not each and every trip, mind you, but sure I've see one. Running up and down the train. Scary as all get out if you ask me!"

They had reached the very back of the train, or the nose of the rear locomotive which had been uncovered. Now, the three boys' attention was fixed on the strange-looking nose of the big locomotive.

It was almost flat with two square windows high up looking a lot like eyes. A company logo crest was affixed below and between them giving the appearance of a nose, with a small air vent set below that as if it were the small mouth.

Pete nudged Jupiter in the ribs. "Hey, First. Did you ever see anything like it?"

Jupiter didn't answer. His attention was fully on the locomotive. He had, in fact, never seen anything like it, not even in books.

"Sir," he asked startling his two friends. "Is this really a

Mongolian locomotive? Not an American one someone cut the heavy front end off of and put on this flat new face?"

Mutters of "What's that kid asking?" and "Is this some sort of put up?" could be heard and the tour guide put his hands on his hips and let out a huffing sound.

"No, kid, this is really a Mongolian train engine, not some sort of hacked together thing." He turned away as if that settled it, but whipped around when an adult voice came from behind the three boys.

"Actually, it is a Chinese locomotive from the Trans-Mongolian Railroad. I've ridden that route several times as part of my job. Runs from Moscow in Russia across parts of Siberia, through the mountains and Gobi Desert in Mongolia and ends in Peking eight or sometimes nine days later. Beautiful scenery all along but deadly cold in the winter." Crowd reaction to this new information prompted him to add, "In winter there are coal fires stoked by hand in each carriage using forced air from outside to circulate heat though the car. If you have a compartment close to the furnace, your room is far too hot to be comfortable unless you open your window… and at the other end it is barely warm enough to get a comfortable night's sleep."

Their guide stood slack-jawed for several seconds. He shook his head as if waking up and cleared his throat.

"Well, that's interesting stuff and I'll be sure to mention it to the Conductor. We might have to change what I tell folks! Ha-ha-ha-ha."

He glanced at the crowd as if judging whether to go on. With a shrug he told them to go ahead and get aboard. "We'll be leaving right on time so don't try going back into the main station. Wouldn't want you to miss out on the experience."

"Aren't you forgetting something, Willard?" a voice came from the door of the car in front of the locomotive. It was a large man wearing the uniform of a train Engineer.

"Huh? Oh, yeah. If you all will come this way and sort of crowd together between the red lines on the ground, we have a little something to show you how serious this Ghost Train is."

People shuffled together until they were in the right places. At that point heavy tarps dropped all around the group right down to the platform. It became very dark and one woman squeaked that she was afraid of the dark that she wanted her husband to hold her. Then, to everyone's delight, she squeaked again complaining that at least three men were now hugging her.

A speaker above them blared out a pre-recorded voice.

"The Ghost Train is about to take you on a trip of a lifetime… or is it?" With that the front tarp, the one closest to the locomotive rose and there was nothing to be see. All was in darkness.

Suddenly, a series of ghostly green neon lights came of outlining the locomotive and a swirling gas descended making it difficult to see the engine. As the neon tubes flickered and then shone hazily, Jupe realized they must be mounted behind semi-opaque glass. It did give the train a ghostly green appearance.

A strobe light mounted high and behind the crowd flashed for about fifteen seconds and then all lights went out.

When they came on, the locomotive was gone!

4
The Journey Begins With a Puzzle

JUPE, TO THE DISMAY of their guide, loudly whispered to Bob and Pete as to how the locomotive disappearance was made to happen.

"It didn't. They did something with the lights and I think another sheet between us and the locomotive. It certainly was something hiding the locomotive, and did you notice the slight bit of steam? All meant to make it seem it went away."

All the lights had gone out again and when they came up the locomotive was back. After that everyone was sent to board the train.

It was well past six before the train finally pulled out from the station in Los Angeles. Some sort of work on the tracks between Palm Springs and Yuma, Arizona, was delaying all eastbound rail traffic.

"It's going to take forever," Bob moaned. He had arranged to be away from his work at the Public Library for only the scheduled seven days of the trip out and flight back into LAX. Now, after an announcement of another one-hour delay it was also made known the trip might take one additional day.

The boys made their way from their cramped room toward the rear of the fifteen-car train and to the buffet or dining car. There they learned that only breakfasts and diners would be at the tables with service. Lunches and all-day snacks would be buffet-style and be self-serve. That suited them just fine as they weren't so much sit-and-dine types as eat-and-go.

While Jupe walked over to and studied the offerings for the afternoon snacks, one of the Stewards came over and began picking up the various trays.

"Huh?" Jupiter muttered. "A fellow just gets to the food when it gets taken away?"

The Steward, a middle-thirties-aged black man looked at him and smiled. "You go ahead and take what you want, young sir. But dinner will start getting served in about an hour. You and your friends," and here he tilted his head toward the waiting Pete and Bob, "got your dinner reservation in?"

"Uhhh, no. We didn't know we had to sign up just to eat."

The man laughed. "Don't gotta sign up if ya want food brought to yer room, but if you want a table, then you gotta get on the list. Just so happens I've got that list right here. Got a table for three at seven and another at seven thirty. Want one of them?"

Jupe decided for the group they would take the earlier sitting and thanked the man, handing him a dollar bill.

"And, I thank you greatly, kind young sir. Anything you want ask fer Joseph, okay?" He smiled a bright smile at Jupe who returned it.

Dinner was an acceptable offering of a rather small steak and a pasta dish that had both small Pacific shrimps in it as well as fresh green peas in a cheesy cream sauce. Dessert was even better as it was fresh berry pie with two scoops of ice cream, one vanilla and the other a mint chocolate chip.

They finished by eight and headed to the observation car and climbed the narrow, spiral stairs up to the row of single seats on the left side. There, they had a backward view of the setting sun as the train headed past the station in Ontario, California.

Half an hour later they agreed they were tired, mostly from all the waiting, and headed to their compartment. The two top bunks were released from the walls and came down on the chains that kept them flat and even. The bottom bunk had been folded down from its normal position as the back of the sofa against the wall it shared with the corridor.

Pete and Bob were glad to take the upper berths as they knew Jupe and his pudgy—or as he called it, "stout" and "non-athletic"—body might have difficulty getting up and into one of the beds now sitting about five feet above the floor.

They got onto pajamas, used the cramped bathroom facilities and got under the covers and were sound asleep before nine thirty.

It was close to midnight when Jupe woke up to the sound of footsteps. Confused, he shook his head and listened carefully. Yes! They were coming not from the corridor but from the roof of the train.

Somebody is up there, he thought with a shiver.

Then, as quickly as it had come, the noise stopped only to be followed by a blast of icy air coming under the door as if someone had opened a door to the outside during a windstorm. Then, it too stopped.

But to Jupe's consternation the footsteps started back up, sounding more like someone jogging down the corridor toward their room. He slipped from bed, yanked his pants partway on and opened the door a crack.

"What's going on?" he demanded of the shadowy figure that had just passed his door. The man turned, looked at Jupe before giving him a shove in the chest—causing Jupe to flounder backwards—and fled the direction he'd been heading.

Knowing that anyone wearing a mask on a train must be up to no good, Jupe pulled on his pants the rest of the way and took off after the man. He heard the door to the next car open and slam closed seconds before he turned the small left then right corners to get to that same door. He took a deep breath hoping the man was not simply waiting between the cars to do him an injury, or worse, and yanked the door open.

Nobody was inside the accordion tunnel between cars.

The noise of the tracks racing below was deafening so he repeated the grab and yank of the next door. It took him two pulls before it moved and slid open revealing the next short corridor and corner.

Again, there was nobody visible, but he could hear the sounds of someone falling over something and then getting up.

As he skidded around the short corner and into the main corridor of the next car a pair of hands reached out and grabbed onto Jupe. He wanted to struggle but quickly focused his eyes on the man in front of him, the man wearing the uniform of the train's Conductor.

"Stop right there, boy!" he ordered in a firm, no-nonsense voice. "There's no running around on this train! And, no running around by youngsters at any time!"

"But I'm chasing that man in the cape!" Jupe protested, but it fell on deaf ears.

"Children like you oughta be with your parents. Now, skedaddle back to whatever compartment you're assigned and don't let me catch you out in these corridors at night for the rest of the trip!"

The First Investigator hated being called a child and disliked to an even greater degree being talked down to as if anything he might engage in was of no importance.

He made a mental note of the man's name tag: E. Donlevy

Holding up an index finger to forestall any further comments from the older man Jupiter reached for his wallet pulling out one of the business cards he and the other two carried. He handed it to the Conductor who read it:

THE THREE INVESTIGATORS

"We Investigate Anything"

?   ?   ?

First Investigator – JUPITER JONES
Second Investigator – PETER CRENSHAW
Records and Research – BOB ANDREWS

With narrowed eyes the older man looked at Jupe and shook his head. He did not ask about the three question marks, and that was Jupe's favorite thing to describe.

"Got a grandson who has one of them little kiddie presses and he makes stuff like this all the time. Don't mean a heck of a lot! Now, get, boy. Do as your elders tell you."

Jupe sighed, held up his finger once again and pulled out two additional slips of paper. The first one was from an old friend, Chief Reynolds of the Rocky Beach Police. He handed it to the man. This one said:

> This certifies that the bearer is a Volunteer Junior Assistant Deputy co-operating with the police force of Rocky Beach. Any assistance given him will be appreciated.
>
> (Signed) Samuel Reynolds Chief of Police.

"I don't know..." the man said slowly reaching out to take the next paper from Jupe. It was something that had arrived a few weeks earlier with a short note stating "This might come in handy someday!" The man's eyes grew wide as he read this one:

> Please let it be known and the three young men

31

referred to in this letter, Jupiter Jones, Robert Andrews and Peter Crenshaw, all of Rocky Beach, California, and known collectively as The Three Investigators, have been instrumental in helping the Federal Bureau of Investigation—whose seal should appear above this letter—in matters regarding National Security and should be afforded cooperation in any investigative endeavor they may be engaged in.

ANTHONY ANDERSON,
Special Agent in Charge

With a slightly shaking hand now, the Conductor handed back the page to Jupe who carefully folded it and put it away.

"In case you were wondering, I'm Jupiter Jones. In case you want to see my identification—"

"No. Don't pull anything more from that wallet of yours. Just tell me what you're doing and we can part quickly. I'm getting a real headache now."

Jupe told the man about the mysterious noises coming from atop the train and then the blast of cold air that raced through the coach before the footsteps had come past his room.

"When I opened the door, there was a figure in a black cape, with a mask over his nose and eyes, sort of like they wear at costume parties, and he looked really angry seeing me there, tried to shove me back into the room, and ran away. I was trying to follow him when you stopped me. Didn't you hear orsee him?"

"Didn't see or hear nothing. Wouldn't have heard nothing 'cause of my headphones. I was listening to some Vivaldi on my Walkman. Sorry, kid... uhhh, I mean Mr Jones. Far as seeing anything, all the racket you were making got me in the corridor in time to catch you. I only saw you."

Not wanting to prolong their conversation any further, and realizing it would be fruitless to point out that whoever made the noise had done so before Jupiter entered that second rail car, he nodded and said he would be heading back to his compartment.

Jupe had a fitful rest of the night and he finally rolled out of his lower bunk at 5:00 heading for the dining car.

The Stewards were just setting the tables but one of them noticed Jupe and came over to ask if he wanted some hot tea or cocoa, "Or something strong like some hot, black coffee?"

"Can I have a hot cocoa with some coffee in it? I need something to knock the cobwebs out of my head."

"Shore. We gots one of those ex-press-o machines so I can make you the cocoa and put a strong shot of coffee in it as well. If that don't wake you up, nothing will." He turned and walked away, cackling as if he'd just said the funniest thing in the world.

Jupe rolled his eyes but sat looking out the window and the dark scenery passing almost invisibly by until the Steward returned, a steaming mug on a small tray.

"Brought ya a small pitcher of milk in case it's too hot and ya want ta cool it down."

Jupe thanked the man and asked for the bill to sign.

"Ah, cocoa's on the house, or on the train, so ta speak. Oh," the man said looking past Jupe. "I think these boys are with you."

Pete and Bob, both looking tired and bleary-eyed sat down, looked at what Jupiter had and asked for the same. "Whatever it is," Pete added.

"So, what the heck had you jump up a couple hours ago, race out of the room and them come back a while later to toss yourself into your bunk" Bob inquired.

Jupe told them about the noises above, the cold air as if a door to the outside had been opened for a moment, then the footsteps outside.

"I tried to follow him as he ran but he got into the next car and made so much noise the Conductor came out and grabbed me as I tried to follow the mystery man."

The only good to come from it was the sight of the man's face on reading the FBI's letter. On hearing about that both of the others smiled.

"It was nice of Agent Anderson to send that letter to us," Pete stated. Bob smiled his agreement. Each of them carried a photostatic copy.

But, Jupiter was glum. "What bothers me is that I had to identify myself and I have no idea if that Conductor will spread it all around that three teenage boys are playing detective on the train. If that happens we might never find out what the heck is going on. Too many people will be on guard."

The Steward returned with two more mugs and two additional small pitchers of milk. He smiled and waived off as they reached out for the bill.

"Well, that is certainly nice of him," Bob said as he tried a sip. He grinned. "Really great cup of cocoa, but there's something else about it. Something with a lot of flavor. Wonder what it is?"

Jupe decided to not tell them about the strong espresso that had been added to their drinks.

He had other things on his mind such as how the man had been on top of the train to begin with and then how he got back inside.

Assuming he came from inside originally, the investigator thought with a cold shiver.

5
The Ghost Makes an Appearance

BY THE time they passed south of Phoenix the next afternoon, the train had gained almost half an hour on its schedule, but this was to shortly be thwarted when a Westbound freight train with priority use of the tracks forced them onto a side rail for nearly fifty minutes.

The Conductor, understanding the frustrations of the passengers, allowed anyone who wished to take a walk to leave the train on the opposite side from the main tracks. He announced the twenty-minute window on the train's PA system and told anyone wishing to remain on board they could claim a free "light adult punch" drink or soda of their choice in the dining car.

"I don't know about you guys," Jupe told his companions, "but I'd like to get a closer look at that secret car up front. I know we can't get into it, but maybe something outside will give us a clue what is in there."

"Bu-but there's gonna be a lot of people out there and I'll bet the Conductor and maybe some other train people too. We'd be seen for sure," Bob said.

Jupe smiled. "Not if we are on the other side of the cars."

Pete was shaking his head. "If you take a look outside there's almost no room between us and any train that passes. We could be hurt or killed. And, I really am not *that* curious."

The First Investigator sighed. He was about to give up the idea when the PA system turned on.

"Uhhh, ladies and gentlemen, this is the Chief Engineer. While we are stopped I have asked our mechanic to open up the diesel engine and take a look at a noisy bearing. Probably nothing but these old girls do have their quirks and I'd hate for us to come to a grinding halt late tonight. It's only gonna take an extra twenty to thirty minutes, depending, so sit tight and I have authorized the dining car staff to provide a free glass of wine or a beer for our adults with your dinner, and for our three teen passengers, a large milkshake or malted. Thanks for your understanding."

Jupe's face split into a huge grin as the oncoming train was announced to pass them in the next five minutes. "Well, isn't that fortuitous," he said to the other Investigators. "I guess we will have some time after all with nothing to *kill* us."

Bob and Pete groaned. They knew that Jupiter sometimes threw caution to the wind in an effort to get to the bottom of a mystery. And, even though this was not an official case with a client or anything close to it, the First Investigator had his "teeth" in it and wasn't about to let go.

Not for the first time Pete thought that Jupe would make a good name for a bulldog.

Their first attempt at getting out on the wrong side was thwarted by the Conductor who was standing by the door of the foremost passenger car, almost as if guarding against the very thing Jupe wanted to do.

"Not this side, boys," he cautioned. "There's barely enough room for the skinny kid to stick his hind end out when the next train comes along, much less yours," he said looking a the somewhat larger form of Jupe.

"Go on back to the other end of this car and you can get out on the right side."

They turned around and headed for the indicated exit. Once on the ground and about half a car away from any other passenger, Jupe bent down and looked under the car. With a satisfied grunt he dropped onto all fours and scurried under the car between the heavy steel wheels.

Once fully under he said, "Keep guard and if the Conductor sees just the two of you tell him I went to our compartment to use the toilet!"

"Jupe!" Pete nearly pleaded. "Come back out of there!"

But, there was no other answer than the sounds of Jupe scooting under and to the other side.

In two minutes he was back again and dusting off his jeans.

"At first our friend was still hanging out of one of the windows, smoking, before he pulled his head inside. Then, that freight train came around the corner and I guess everyone was right. If I'd been standing there, even pushed up against the train, I'd have been a goner."

"Giving up then?" Bob inquired.

"Not by a long shot. We'll just have to do it at night when everyone other than the Engineer are asleep."

Neither Bob nor Pete took comfort from Jupe's statement.

By the time the train started moving again, they had been back inside for almost forty minutes.

"I don't like this," complained Bob, "That delay is going to mean I'll get back two days late and the Head Librarian only agreed to let me take time off if I'd get back in no more than eight days." He looked sad. "I'll lose my job now."

"What if you call and tell him this is a breakdown and not you trying to get more days off?"

Bob looked at Jupe. He shook his head. "You think he's going to believe a teenager who only works twenty-two hours a week. Ha!"

Jupe didn't like to think his ideas weren't top-notch, so he responded, "What if an adult called him? What if it was a train company employee. Well?"

Bob didn't look convinced but he said, "Maybe. But, who?"

When dinner time came around, the boys headed for the dining car having signed up for early sittings all through the journey. It was something Jupe enjoyed but had to admit that by ten or so at night his stomach was asking him where the late snack might be coming from.

They had no sooner placed their orders with Steward Joseph Miller than a well-dressed woman got up from a table halfway down the car and approached them with a concerned look on her face. It was one Jupe had seen far too many times.

"Pardon me, but it appears that you children don't have an adult with you. Or, is your mommy or daddy just staying in your compartment?"

Jupe who hated being called a child or "kid" looked at her and put his sad face on. "I am sorry to tell you, old woman, that my *mother* and *father* perished in an automobile accident when I was but a young boy of four. Now that I am a teen, I live with relatives who did not choose to make this journey as they believe in my ability to take a simple train trip without supervision. And that is because they trust me and my friends here," he looked at Pete and Bob, "to make this journey without them. But, thank you for your concern. I'm certain your own grandchildren appreciate your loving ways." He smiled at her in a dismissive way.

The woman stood up straight and made a huffing sound. "Well, I've never. I do not have grandchildren for your information. I am only forty-nine years old. The nerve!" and she whisked away back to the table where a rather amused man was sitting trying not to laugh.

She swatted his forearm and he broke up into gales of laughter.

So did most of the people who had witnessed her

interaction with the Investigators.

"That was certainly worth the ticket price," whispered the man who was fast becoming their favorite server in the dining car. He set down their salads and moved off to the next table.

After dinner they spent an hour in the observation car before heading to bed. Bob and Pete pulled out novels they'd brought to wile away some time. Jupe had brought no reading materials, but had brought along a small playing card deck-sized box he took out and began working on.

"What is that?" Pete asked looking down at Jupe's bunk.

"Huh? Oh, this is a special little gizmo I have been tinkering with for a month or more. It's a camera that attaches to anything metallic, or at least that has steel or iron in it, and once set for a specific time it takes up to twenty pictures at between two and ten-second intervals."

"Neat," exclaimed his curious friend. "Two questions. Why, and do you have to take it to a drug store to get it developed?"

"The why," Jupe told him sounding as if it ought to be obvious, "is because I want to see if we can get some proof there is someone in the corridor at night who should not be there. As to developing..." he reached into his duffel bag and pulled out a black plastic canister. "I brought along my portable developing kit. We can't get prints but I can develop the negatives in about fifteen minutes!"

Bob had poked his head over his bunk, now interested. "What if the phantom of whatever comes along before or after you set that to go off?"

Jupe's grin told them both he had more information to impart.

"I can also rig it to work on a trip wire. I'm going to place it above our door in a couple hours and set the wire across the floor in front of the door. It is not a trip-and-pull wire, it is a step on and break sort so he should have no idea he's started the thing working."

There had been no footsteps outside their door by eleven and so Jupe got up and opened the door. With Bob climbing onto his shoulders, the other boy managed to attach the box to the ceiling with its fisheye lens pointing downward able to catch images below and out to either end of the hall.

He came down with the thin wire in his fingers and handed it to Jupe. It was a matter of seconds to put another small object, this time a miniature pulley, on one side of the corridor and something looking like an eye-bolt across from it. The wire was strung through the pulley and attached to the eye where it was pulled taut causing the box above to emit a single click.

"That sets it for immediate use once it has been tripped. And I set the timing for two-second internal shots."

Try as they might to remain awake, by midnight the boys were all asleep with Jupiter slightly snoring. None of them became aware of the noises in the corridor at 2:00 am when something making a zinging noise passed by their door followed by footsteps and a man's voice giving a hoarse, "Damn!" as it passed.

Before going to breakfast Jupe and Bob retrieved the camera box and the two lower devices. It was obvious the tripwire had been broken and Jupe hoped they got some good pictures. He'd outfitted the camera with very fast film so even in the nighttime low light of the passageway he believed they would see something.

With an hour to go before breakfast service he hastily pulled out a special thick black cloth bag that would let no light inside, put the developing tank and his camera into it, and began moving his hands all around. Ten minute later his face changed from one of concentration to happiness.

"Got it! Now for the developing liquids.

He pulled the tank out and unscrewed a special cap on top and then the top of a separate pint bottle. This he tipped above the tank pouring in all the liquid. Once it had been recapped he began turning a small handle looking at his watch every minute or so until ten minutes had passed.

The liquid was drained back into the bottle and then replaced by what he called a "stop bath," and the turning began anew for five minutes this time. Once the stop bath was removed he took the tank to their small sink and filled it with clean water which he cranked around for two minutes, replace with more clean water and another two minutes and then drained fully.

He pulled the strip of film out and clipped it to the edge of Pete's bunk sitting over a small hand towel.

"By the time we get back from breakfast, he announced, "the film will be dry and we can touch it."

When they did get back to the room thirty-two minutes later the film had nearly dried, but it was enough to let Jupe pick it up and hold it to the light.

"Yes!" he shouted. The others crowded around him and he showed them the images. It was all in opposites; blacks were white and white were black, but they could tell some of the details.

There was the top of a head of a man, unrecognizable, in the first frame who then moved about fifteen feet down the corridor to where something looking an awful lot like a cartoon ghost was. They could see him grabbing and trying to move it—or choke it, which is what it really appeared to be—in frames four through eleven before whatever it was disappeared quickly down the passage in the following two frames with the man heading that way as well.

Frames fourteen on were just the corridor.

"That doesn't look like a very interesting ghost," Pete stated.

"And, that doesn't look at all like the phantom man I saw and chased," Jupe told them.

It was becoming curiouser and curiouser!

6
Night Two and Another Encounter

THEY SPENT most of the next day in either the observation car or the dining car. Both had excellent views but the dining car had the advantage of allowing them to look over every person who came through, and that included just about every passenger at some point and many of the crew. It also gave them access to food the minute it was brought out.

But, to Jupe's way of thinking, the bonus on all this was he got to spend some time talking to the different members of the train staff from the Mechanic—who turned out to have been the train guide on day one—to the Chief Engineer.

Each had varying stories about the origins of the train, but the Chief Engineer was most interested in Jupe's recently-obtained knowledge of the rear locomotive engine.

In a very low voice, the man admitted, "We sort of made up all that jazz about the engine having been unclaimed. The fact is the owner of this train special ordered it from a salvage company in China. The only thing he didn't want were the three dead people that were really in there when they opened it up. That part is true and gave him the idea this is a ghost haunted train. And, I suppose it is!"

He caught the expectant look in their eyes. "You guys want a private tour of the engine at the back?" When they practically shouted, but did not, he got up. "Well, come on, then. I'm supposed to be on my sleep break, but I'll give you a good look at it all for a couple minutes."

They passed through the private crew car and saw that there were three doors along the passageway.

"Sleeping quarters, refrigerated food and head," he told

them as he unlocked the door at the very back. When Pete asked who's head, the Engineer chuckled and explained he was referring to a bathroom

The first thing they saw as they crowded inside the rear end of the locomotive car was a wide hammock strung between stanchions on the right side of the engine room.

"I used to be in the Navy and on a really old ship that still had some of these. My bed was one of them and I have trouble sleeping in anything else. I put in ear plugs and the engine noise lulls me to sleep. Don't tell anyone, but we give the regular passengers a bit of a story about it being one of the places a skeleton was discovered!"

He showed them how the diesel engine was spit between a right and left sides with an elevated walkway in between. "The ten cylinders were in surprisingly good condition. The real engineering feat was when the owner discovered the gauge of the tracks in Russia and Mongolia was wider than our standard gauge. Four foot and something like eleven-and-twenty-seven thirty-seconds versus our scale of four foot eight and a half inches."

"I guess he was furious about the extra costs," Bob suggested.

"You know, you'd think so but he got this thing for a song so a few extra thousand bucks to pull the original trucks, that's the wheel groups, and replace them with surplus American ones didn't seem to bother him. The important thing was the power connections all could be moved and bolted together strong and tight."

He told them the original idea was to have a different locomotive back at the end, another one by the same manufacturer as the one in front, Fairbanks-Morse.

"That fell through because the only one still in existence *and* for sale—they built just fifty-nine of 'em—was a rust-bucket on wheels sitting outside in Atlanta, Georgia. Sweet little engine called the Baby Train Master." He stopped talking as if the thought of that locomotive was a fond memory.

Next they went to the front of the locomotive where he opened the door to the controller's room.

The instruments were fairly dirty and a few featured broken glass.

"We sort of control everything from the other end so we never did fully restore this room," he admitted.

"What if you had to use it?" Jupe asked. "Such as if you overshoot a station and have to back up?"

"Then, the Chief Mechanic comes back here with a radio and directs me up front. It's happened a couple times when the linkage to this end had, umm, problems and kept pushing when it should have been braking. Never overshot anything by more than a couple hundred yards, but it's a good question."

Ten minutes later after demonstrating a few of the features of this locomotive that were not found in domestic units, he apologized but stated he had to get some sleep.

"Just shut the door to the main part of the train when you go through the sleeping car," he requested before showing them out the back of the Mongolian engine.

Jupe was all for staying in the private car and seeing if they could get into the sleeping quarters but Bob and Pete pushed him forward and soon they were out of the car and into the observation car.

Straightening his shoulders with a "hmmmmph!" sound he asked, "Now, why did you both shove me out? Huh? I bet we could have found out some interesting things."

"I'll bet," Pete stated using his head to indicate the

Conductor who was coming their way, "we could have got caught!" he ended in a whisper.

Sure enough, the Conductor touched the brim of his cap before pulling out a set of keys on a long retractable cable. A few seconds later he was through the locked door.

"Okay. We ducked a bad one there," Jupe admitted.

They headed back to the dining car and the table they'd left twenty minutes earlier. It had been cleaned of any indication anyone had been sitting there.

Their favorite Steward came out of the side kitchen area.

"Oh, you're back I see. Thought you'd headed out for the time. Want some more sodas and another bowl of chips?"

"That'd be great!" Bob said.

"Yeah, but I have to go to the bathroom," Pete explained.

Jupe nodded. "I think we all might do that. We'll be back in ten minutes."

Okay," the Steward told them setting down a bowl he'd just picked up along with a RESERVED sign for the table.

When the boys got back it was Jupe who reached for the potato chips first and came up with a small, folded note.

"Odd," he said opening it. His eyes went wide and his jaw dropped. "Get this," he hissed and read the note out loud:

Nosey little kids can find themselves in some very deep and hot water. Stop snooping or else!

"What's that all about?" Bob asked.

"What else," Jupe said with a small smile. "We've touched some nerves and someone wants us to stop. I say we ignore this note and really look into this. We need to set up a rotation so one of us will be awake at night. Probably best to do this in two-hour shifts."

That night after a nice dinner of some roast pork with gravy, mashed red potatoes and fresh green beans, the boys went to their compartment.

"What was with those beans?" Pete asked.

"What was with them was they were fresh and not those horrible canned things you eat at your house. Anyway," Jupe said determined to get their lookout schedule agreed to, "We seem to want to drop off by around 10:00, so I'll take the first watch before waking Bob at midnight, and then he wakes you, Pete, at 2:00, then at 4:00 I'm back up, Bob at 6:00 and then Pete starts tomorrow night, Okay?"

It seemed to be acceptable to the others.

Nothing happened during Jupe's watch.

Nothing happened during Bob's watch either.

And Pete almost skated by with nothing occurring when at twenty minutes to 4:00 Pete knew he had been lightly dozing but a sudden draft of cold air coming into the compartment from the corridor woke him up fully.

He quietly slid to the floor and placed his right ear to the door. He could hear sounds of heavy breathing and slow, deliberate footsteps.

Without thinking he slid the door open and stepped into the passage.

Lugging an evidently heavy bag down the corridor was a black-clad figure.

With his entire body tingling in fear, Pete said, "Wh-wh-what the h-heck is g-g-goin on?"

The figure that Pete thought must be seven feet tall turned and dropped the bag.

"In yer room, boy, or you're a dead man!" he hissed with menace dripping from each syllable. Then, the man lunged toward Pete who skidded backwards into the Investigators' compartment and leaned heavily against the door as he sought to find the lock.

As it finally snapped shut, both Bob and Jupe woke with a start.

"What happened?" Jupe asked getting his voice first.

"M-m-m-man. Out-t th-there!" Pete said pointing over his shoulder. "Bl-black cape and a big bag."

Jupe had already jumped out of his bunk and was trying to get past Pete who was in no frame of mind to be of assistance. By the time the First Investigator got the door unlocked and open, there was no sight of the man. He raced forward and opened the doors into the next car and ran around the corner and right into the arms of the Conductor.

The man looked at Jupe in surprise.

Jupe looked at him and then past him, seeing nobody else in the passageway.

"Yeah," he said in a sad voice, "I know. Go to bed, kid!" He turned to leave but the Conductor placed a large hand on his shoulder.

"Yes," he said in a level voice, "You go to bed, but this time I have to say I heard something going on out here about twenty seconds before you came around that corner. I saw nothing by the time I got out here, but now I think I might believe that you did hear something the other night. Still, I have to tell you this is not anything a passenger should be involved in. Now, good night!" he said and his eyes told Jupe the man was convinced and was doing his job in telling the boys to butt out.

7
Ghost Train on the Move

Before anybody else woke up and headed for the dining car that morning, the train pulled into El Paso, Texas, one of the stations where they would be allowed off the train for several hours.

The three took turns in the tiny combination toilet and shower before getting dressed and heading down the train to get something to eat. It had been hardest on Jupe whose size meant he could barely turn around when it came time to rinse off.

No stores would be open for at least another hour so they had time to sit and talk about what they wanted to do.

Jupe, always the best prepared, pulled out three brochures.

"There aren't a lot of things to see other than art museums that are within good walking distance or that we could see and still be back by noon," he told them.

They decided even the Fort Bliss military museum would not be a good idea as the brochure said to allow at least five hours to see everything.

Closing the last brochure, Jupe sighed. "I guess this means just walking around the downtown area and seeing what we might find."

Pete and Bob agreed. They also agreed they need not wait until shops opened. It was going to be an eight block walk to get to the edge of downtown El Paso anyway, so they gulped down their bowls of cereal and left after grabbing Bob's fancy 35mm camera and several rolls of film.

"Did you bring just the film in your camera gadget, Jupe, or is there more in your bag?" Bob inquired as they headed across the tracks and out of the station.

"I brought three packs of film plus the one that was in the camera, but I can make more from any roll of 35mm film as long as I have a dark room and a pair of scissors. It uses the film split down the middle and a small battery to turn a cogged wheel. And, I also brought more batteries."

"Why didn't we bring the film and get prints made?" Pete asked.

"Same reason regarding splitting the film down the middle. No photo house can do a good job with that off-sized film unless you give them a couple days. We have a couple hours so I'll have to wait until we get home to make large prints."

Crossing the first street Bob asked Jupe what he thought of the bits they could make out on the small film strip.

"This one isn't at all like that case with what we thought might be ghosts in the attic of that cranky old man, Mr Pilcher," Jupe asserted. "I mean, at first we thought it might be invisible. This man in black with the cape is anything but invisible and also anything but insubstantial. When I tackled him, or tried to, there was solid human in there!

"This new thing in the pictures seems to be a case of a mechanical ghost misbehaving, perhaps during a test run, and its minder having to give it a good shake to free it up, them it whipped away as fast as can be."

"Thought it would be something like that," Bob said with a grin that said he'd never had that thought at all!

They walked up one street before turning to the right at a baseball stadium then continuing along West Missouri Avenue until it turned, for no good reason they could see, into East Missouri Avenue. A couple blocks later the small guidebook they had picked up from the train station said to turn right on North Stanton, which they did. Within a couple more blocks they realized this was probably the city center and so they began to look at the various storefronts.

Although larger than their own Rocky Beach it was more like the sort of downtown Santa Monica might have been if the area had not been turned into a tourist town. This was definitely not a tourist town; it was a no-nonsense downtown the sort you could find in hundreds of mid-sized American cities.

It was also not a very tall downtown coming in at about seven stories at its tallest.

Jupe noticed with some interest there were a fair number of places to eat and an even larger number of bars and taverns including a couple advertising "Family Friendly Atmosphere!" nearby signs stating "Over 21 Only!"

"I'm glad this is only a five hour stopover," Pete stated. "This place is kind of creepy. Have you noticed there aren't all that many people or cars around and it is going on start of the workday?"

Most of the stores seemed, for no truly good reason other that the state in which they were located, to be very Texas-centric. Everywhere they looked were displays of cowboy clothing, hats, boots and even two saddle shops.

The store that made them laugh the most was a travel agency advertising "A wide range of exciting getaways!" along with a window display of some of the items of clothing they also sold for such vacations. Everything either had leather fringe on it or was embroidered with images of cows and cowboy with lariats.

"I guess these folks don't like to feel they're leaving Texas at home if they go places like..." and Jupe paused as he tapped one place on the large front window, "...Tahiti. Nothing says getting down and comfortable on a hot, tropical island like a leather vest that says, 'Proud to be a Texan!' I suppose there is something to say for being proud of where you come from."

Bob was shaking his head. "Not if you don't want to stand out like a mudball in a punchbowl," he said pointing at a poster of the Eiffel Tower with a trio of cowboy-dressed women standing there smiling. To make matters worse, none of them had what might be though of as an honest smile looking rather pained to be standing around in heavy boots, leather skirts and leather jackets over gaudy plaid shirts complete with string ties on what appeared to be a very hot mid-summer day.

With a shrug they moved on.

"Uh, fellow," Jupe whispered, "I don't want to alarm you, and don't look around—! Ah, Pete," he moaned as the boy whipped his head right then left trying to see what Jupe might have. "I swear. If you were on the battlefield and your sergeant yelled, 'Duck!' you'd stand there looking up going, 'I don't see a duck' just before you got shot!"

"Sorry, Jupe," the boy said. "I didn't think it would be wrong to want to see whatever it was."

"Well," Jupiter said as he tried to spot the individual he'd seen in the reflection of a store window they were passing, "perhaps it wasn't a dire thing, but next time please listen to me? I thought I spotted one of the Stewards from the train standing across the street right behind us watching us. He's ducked into the alley over there you can see in the window… Pete! Now is not the time to test my patience. Turn back around."

The boy was bright red at having not thought things through before turning back to the street.

"Let's just amble back that other way and hope he was just curious to see if he knew us." Jupe led them back up South Stanton and the way they had come. He led them to the left on Overland and almost pushed them into a Mexican restaurant on the corner. While Bob and Pete got a table for them he kept watch.

Five minutes passed, and then five more went to join those with no sight of the Steward so Jupe gave up with a shrug and joined the others. Waiting for him was a mug of cocoa and a short stack of pancakes that had just been delivered.

They ate in near silence and left half an hour later once Jupe had stepped outside and to the corner to look all around.

"I'm not feeling a whole lot of love for El Paso," Jupe told them, "so I suggest since we only have three hours, let's get back to the train."

The agreed and all set off back toward the station.

The trio soon crossed Oregon Street and kept going straight, but a noise coming from a very narrow gap between the first and second building had them stopped.

A gun was pointing at them from the deep shadows and a voice growled, "Get in here! NOW!!"

Jupe stepped in first hoping the other two would turn and run while he blocked their attacker, but Bob and Pete dutifully followed him in. For his going in first Jupe took the butt of the gun to his right temple first followed quickly by Bob and then Pete getting the same treatment.

It instantly became the dark of night in the space.

Bob was the first to stir. He groaned before reaching up to find that his head had not been split open, but did have a small cut just above the hairline that had bled. He figured they had been there a while since the blood was nearly dry.

Must have been within the past hour, he thought as he lightly shook Pete, the closest one to him.

"Headache, Mom. Not going to school today," the boy moaned and tried to roll away. His eyes flashed open from the sudden pain the movement caused. "What happened?"

Bob was reaching over him to shake Jupe.

"I'm awake and have been for ten minutes," he grumbled. "I hope you enjoyed the nap because the train was supposed to leave fifteen minutes ago. I figured that if we were going to miss it, I might just as well let you wake up on your own."

They helped each other to stand and brush off their dusty clothing before stepping out into the light of day. The glare hurt almost as much as the impact points on their heads.

"Let's get to the station and see what can be done," Pete suggested so they headed back to the train depot. To all their surprises the Ghost Train was right there as if it was waiting for them to get back. The sight of it made them hustle faster and soon they were on the platform entering their car.

All three went to their compartment where they splashed water in their faces and cleaned up a little blood that marked where each had taken the hit.

The Ghost Train will leave the El Paso station in five minutes. This is a recorded departure announcement.

Jupe groaned. He just realized that he had not set his watch with the change from Mountain Zone time to Central Zone and it was now a full behind rather than being correct.

As the train lurched slightly and got on the move, he decided that unless one of the others asked, he would not mention that little fact.

8

The Trans-Texas Crossing Incident

THE BOYS decided to keep a low profile the rest of the day. A good nap seemed called for so they requested sandwiches be delivered for dinner and settled in to sleep by about noon.

When the knock came on their door at 6:45, Jupe answered it hoping against hope it would not be the Steward he'd seen behind them and who presumably had attacked them. Of course he could not be sure which one it had been as the man had been at least sixty feet away and reflected poorly in the early morning light. Besides, all the stewards were young to 30-ish aged black men so skin tone would be no help.

To his great surprise, the Steward turned out to be a young black woman.

She started to hand him the tray but stopped and looked at his face.

"You hurt, sir?" she asked. "I only mention it because you got a little trickle of dry blood on your forehead. None of my business so you can just say, 'Ellie, darlin'. Ain't none of your business,' and I'll go away."

Jupe touched the place and felt the very dry blood.

"No, that's okay. Just had a little accident while in town. Nothing to worry about and nothing to even mention to anyone. Okay?" He looked at her hopefully

"Sure. Like I said, none of my business. Just put the tray out here when you are finished with it. Someone'll come by in an hour or so."

"Uh, can I ask you a question?" She nodded. "I thought all the Stewards were men. You are obviously a woman, so I was curious." He felt himself turning bright red and silently prayed she wouldn't be insulted.

"I ain't no Steward. I'm the chef on this train. Just happens I got curious about three growing teenage boys all alone on the train so I decided to make the food and bring it to you. As to the 'you're a woman,' I thank you for noticing. Not too many working this place seem to remember I am. You have a nice evening."

She turned and headed back to the dining car.

When the stout Investigator turned around it was to see his companions laying face down on their bunks, chins resting on their hands with goofy grins on their faces.

"Think she's cute, Jupe?" Bob asked.

"Did you want to ask her out on a date?" Pete practically purred.

"Shut up the both of you!" he told them. "She's got to be at least twenty-five! Far too old for me." But, deep inside he had to admit she was a very attractive woman and only about ten years wasn't all that much a gap in their ages. Mentally he shook himself for being a fool and took his sandwich from the tray telling the others to come down and eat on the fold out table.

They ate, set the tray outside as directed, and then everyone climbed back in their bunks and fell asleep again in minutes.

Jupe dreamed of both the attack and the pretty chef, and woke up in a sweat when the chef's pretty face turned into their attacker's face. It so horrified him that he couldn't get back to sleep for more than two hours.

By sun-up the train was passing through Alpine, Texas, a small town with a three-way split in the tracks with one of the tracks passing a railway station set back about twenty feet from the tracks and a flagpole set out with a pennant people could run up if they wanted the train to stop and pick them up. But, as this was a private train they passed right on by and were out of the town limits a half minute later.

Five minutes went by before they were slowing down and the announcement was made that they would be spending about fifteen minutes on a siding while the regular AMTRAK Sunset Limited train—a faster service—would be allowed to pass.

As the other train went by, the Ghost Train shook and shimmied a little in the slipstream, but in seconds it was over and then began moving again almost immediately.

The scenery was uninspiring as the day went on or at least until they passed the town of Sanderson. After that, they began seeing green rather than gray and brown hills around them.

Being from California where green is to be found just about everywhere you don't see ocean, the starkness of this middle area of Texas was... disturbing. They also found the tracks were heading more north for a few miles before swinging back to the east.

The excitement outside ran out about sundown when it was announced there was a mechanical issue with the front locomotive and they needed to travel at half speed. They would not get to San Antonio until very late the following evening. With San Antonio now some thirty-eight hours ahead, Bob became despondent.

"I've as good as lost my job for sure!" he moaned.

Because of needed repairs the San Antonio stop would be the whole scheduled ten hours so passengers would be able to devote the day to sightseeing possibilities. An air of disappointment descended on most of the passengers after the announcement.

But, it was to be replaced by a new level of excitement in all but three of the passengers when, at precicely midnight, a woman's piercing scream came from outside the compartment door, with the screamer continuing making the noise and running down the corridor toward the back of the train.

Doors were yanked open and angry voices demanded to know "What the devil / blazes / heck / is going on!?"

Soon footsteps pelted down the passage and the sound of the interconnect doors opening and closing could be heard from both ends of the car.

Jupe, Pete and Bob hurriedly got dressed and followed about a dozen adults all heading to the back of the train.

In the dining car a ghost-white woman sat panting as one of the Stewards was trying to get her to take a silver flask, presumably one filled with alcohol to steady her nerves.

Just as the boys pushed their way between several upset adults she gasped out, "I saw it! The ghost. I saw it!"

Jupe sputtered and said aloud before he could stop himself, "Oh, well if that's all this is about I'm back to bed!"

"How can you be so damn casual about this?" she asked him in a pleading tone. "It brushed right over my face and I could feel death!"

Jupe shrugged. "We've seen worse," he declared before pushing his way back through the still gathering crowd.

When one angry man grabbed Bob's sleeve and demanded to know what could be worse, the boy looked at him sadly and proclaimed, "We've seen dead bodies before. *Real* dead bodies. A little wispy ghost on a tourist train ain't nothin'!"

9

The Investigators Get Dumped

LATE THAT night, while the sun was still missing from the sky, it was Bob who heard the sounds outside their door. A sort of scraping as if someone was dragging one of their feet along, or something in a bag.

He eased his covers back, swung his legs over his bunk and swiveled around so he could climb down to the floor. The linoleum was installed over steel deck plates so the floor was as cold as it was outside, and that was only about forty degrees.

Bob pulled on his jeans and sweatshirt before opening the door as quietly as he could.

He stepped out into the corridor just in time to see a dark shape, someone wearing what looked like a cape, disappearing around the front end of the car. He raced down the corridor and reached the far end as the door to the next car snapped shut with a loud *click.*

Bob reached out and yanked the handle down, pulling the door to the side as hard as he could. As he reached the other door handle something began nagging at the back of his mind.

The other door hadn't clicked shut!

He opened it only to find the Conductor standing in his way. He was smoking a cigarette even though that was against the law and, as many signs told passengers, it was punishable by a $500 fine.

"Where did he go?" Bob demanded.

Turning his head and blushing at having been caught, the Conductor asked, "Who? Where did who go?"

Bob let out a strangled scream, turned around and headed back to bed.

But, Jupe and Pete were up and standing in the corridor waiting to see where their friend might have gotten to.

He told them of the noises and his short and unfruitful chase. He also told them the Conductor was smoking inside the train.

"I could smell the smoke on his clothing," he said. "He must sneak a lot of smokes during the day."

Jupe's eyes narrowed. "Did you detect the smell of smoke in the corridor as you followed the phantom?"

Bob slowly shook his head, "You know something, I didn't. It didn't register in my nose until I opened the door in the next car. Hmmm?"

It was just turning 5:00 in the morning but the boys decided to head for the dining car. It was empty so they sat down to wait. Coming into the car five minutes later was Joseph, their favorite Steward.

"Morning, all," he greeted them with a smile on his face. "You're up early again. Gimme a few minutes to get the coffee machine going and I'll fix you some of my special hot cocoas."

"Hey, Joseph," Jupe called out to the man as he headed for the kitchen area.

"Yeah?"

"Just a question. You were coming from the front of the train. I thought you all slept in that last car at the back."

The man smiled. "Not a question, young sir. More a statement. And, you're right. I had to speak with the Conductor so I headed to his compartment a bit ago."

"I thought it was something like that. Thanks, and a bit

extra coffee in mine today. Thanks!"

After an extra large breakfast at 6:30, the boys headed for the upper deck of the observation car where they spent most of the morning and afternoon watching the scenery slowly flow past. They saw large herds of grazing cattle that gave way to mountains with hundreds of goats standing on outcroppings of rocks warily eyeing the train as it passed through their territory.

Dinner was a little late when it was discovered that one of the compressed propane cylinders in the kitchen had a faulty valve.

Everyone was sent to the fifth car or farther forward to wait until the maintenance man gave the all clear word.

The three teens piled into their bunks at nine, dead tired from having been up most of the previous night. It was past midnight before any of them even stirred.

Jupe's right eye, the one now hidden deep in his pillow, opened. There had been a noise that just did not seem right. It was still there, or rather it wasn't there.

The noises of the wheels' *clackity-clacking* over the tracks was missing. It was just too darned quiet.

He slipped out from his covers and went to the door. His heart nearly skipped a beat and someone knocked on it just as his hand touched the handle.

"Wh-wh-what is it? I-I mean, who is it?" he said in a loud whisper, his mouth an inch from the door.

"It's the Conductor," came a hoarse whisper. "We've got a problem and need to get everyone off the train until it is fixed. Very dangerous! Come on out and take the first door outside. Hurry now!"

Then the man must have moved on.

Jupe was so worried about what might be happening he

failed to register the man did not knock on the door next to theirs. He was busy waking his companions.

"Come on, fellows. We have to get off the train, The Conductor just said there's a dangerous problem. Wake up!"

Bob and Pete sleepily dropped to the floor and pulled their pants and shirts on. Jupe hadn't thought of that so he grabbed his plus his shoes and socks and the trio opened the door and walked into the corridor.

Deep in a shadow caused by only one small light being on behind him, the Conductor had just opened the side door and pointed to it.

"Quickly now!" he ordered them and in seconds they were sitting on a small rise about fifty feet form the train pulling on their shoes.

"What the—" Bob exclaimed as the door slammed shut and the train began pulling forward. "Come on. There's nobody else out here. We've been duped!"

But, all three stumbled over some rocks between them and the tracks and by the time they were beside the train, it was moving too quickly to try to jump up and grab a door handle.

Sixty seconds later, the lights of the rear locomotive headed around a bend in the tracks taking any sound with them, and the boys were alone in the dark.

Jupiter let out a sigh. "I'm now thinking that wasn't the Conductor after all. Perhaps it was the man in the cape I've tried to follow a couple times."

"Yeah," Pete agreed, "the ghost! But no matter who he is, he managed to get us off the train without resorting to violence."

Jupe snorted in between puffing from the short run. "Small consolation." He sighed. "As much as I hate the idea of more exercise on almost no sleep, I think we need to head that way.

The last station is five hours back the way we came, and that's at train speed." He pointed the same direction the train had disappeared.

The boys walked several miles along a gravel-bottom ditch running within twenty feet of the train tracks. Jupe was about to give up and sit down when they all felt a rumble beneath their feet.

They were just passing a thick, metal pole at the top of which was one of the infrequent signal light arrangements when Pete saw it.

"Lights!" he exclaimed excitedly.

"We need to get closer to the track," Bob stated. "They might miss us in the dark unless we are really close."

Jupe wasn't so sure it was a good idea to get too close, but he agreed they needed to be seen by whatever this train was coming down the tracks. It was still a few miles away but appeared to be coming fast.

What seemed like a long time later, but must have been only a couple minutes, the train raced past them, all outside lights ablaze, even the green neon ones supposedly only used in stations. It made it difficult to focus on the train and gave everything a ghostly appearance.

"It's our train!" Pete yelled as it thundered past. As suddenly as the rear locomotive engine passed them they all heard the squeal of the brakes being applied and the engines—front and back—being set into reverse.

It finally came to a halt a half mile beyond them, then slowly came back toward them stopping when the fifth car was even with them.

"There you are!" the Conductor exclaimed leaning out of the doorway at the back of that car. "What in the name of Satan possessed you boys to jump off the train?"

"You ought to know!" Pete declared hotly. "You tricked us into getting off and then got the train moving again!"

Jupe was about to also accuse the man when the train's chief Engineer appeared coming down the corridor from the front of the train.

"Can any of you give me a good explanation of what happened and just why you did it?" he demanded.

Bob and Pete looked at the First Investigator who raised a hand and then drew himself up to his full five-foot-seven height.

"If you will listen with an open mind I can tell you exactly what happened, sir." Then, he recounted having been awakened by the lack of noise and movement, the knock on he door and someone telling them they had to leave the train.

"Then it just pulled away and we were far enough to the side we couldn't catch it. But, why did you come back for us?"

"We had a report from a woman in the car behind yours saying she believed someone had been attempting to hop a ride on the train. Hobos, or so she believed. We frown on that but we also have had a previous problem where a passenger was attacked and robbed then pushed out of her window. She survived but we knew nothing about it until the next morning when her traveling companion reported her missing."

"I see," Jupe said slowly. "So, you just decided to put things in reverse?"

"No, son. I had the Conductor here do a headcount. We found your room door ajar and you weren't inside. He put three and three together and called me to say he believed you had left the train when we stopped to replace that faulty engine bearing. Now, since you are juveniles, we are responsible for your welfare so I naturally came back."

"Naturally," said Jupe in a tone that said he didn't believe it for a minute. "Can't have the kids getting lost or killed. Spooked by a phantom dark ghost being that nobody else sees and you all deny, but not harmed." He turned and trudged over to the door and hoisted himself up and inside.

Pete and Bob shrugged, stared at the Conductor who was standing there looking as if he'd been found with his hand in the cookie jar, and followed their friend.

10
Jupe Tails a Man

IT WAS a busy day once the train pulled into San Antonio. People practically shoved each other out of the way to try to get the first taxis to the various tourist destinations.

The boys held back, still slightly wary of heading into a strange town after their El Paso clobbering.

"What do we want to do?" Pete asked.

Jupe's face said he'd like to find the entire train empty and take a look into any place they could open. What he said was, "Let's go to The Alamo and see if it is as impressive as people say. I was a great fan of Davey Crocket on TV as a kid, so this ought to be interesting. Besides," and he let out a sigh, "it is doubtful we can get into any dangerous situation in a taxi or on a bus and then out in the open."

The first two taxis said they were only interested in longer trips and pointed over their shoulders to cars behind them.

The third driver they approached was happy to take them.

"It's kind of a long trip," he cautioned them. "Maybe ten bucks or so." Jupe could tell by the man's shifty eyes he was not telling the truth.

"Really, really long drive, huh?" The driver nodded but looked around to make sure nobody could overhear them. "Longer than the twelve blocks the brochure on the train says?" He looked as innocent as possible, a skill he'd gained as a child actor.

"Umm, yeah. You see what with one way streets and all..." He faltered now and looked defeated as a police officer walked behind them. "No, I was just kidding ya. Just wanting

67

to lighten the mood. Welcome to San Antonio, Texas, and my cab. It is really fourteen blocks and I'll take you all there as straight as I can. No hard feelings over the little joke?"

"Let's all laugh," Jupe said in a slightly sour voice. He looked at his companions and nodded.

"Ha-ha-ha," they all said.

The cab driver opened the rear door for them and after they climbed in he closed it before getting into the driver's seat.

It was a fast drive and the fare was just a dollar, but Jupiter gave the man two and told him to keep the change.

The man stared at the large tip and shrugged. "Hey, thanks, young man." With that he put the cab in gear and sped away before Jupe might change his mind and ask for some money back.

The Alamo turned out to be both incredibly boring and interesting. The building was surrounded by many trees, still fairly young, that the guide told their group had been planted as part of a city beautification project.

"It was a sore point for the purists and historians as this area was pretty much surrounded by cactus and low brush most of the year. But, isn't it pretty?"

"Not really," piped up a man Jupe recognized from the train. It was the same man who had been laughing at his wife over her attempts to talk down to the boys the other evening.

She had evidently heard that reaction before because she shrugged and gave a resigned grin before starting walking to the left side of the little plaza in front of the Alamo building.

The tour lasted only about twenty minutes before their guide announced that they would be allowed a few minutes to peek inside the big doors of the historical site.

"Nobody will be allowed inside, and we ask that you not use flash cameras to take any pictures, but you will be able to see a little of how cramped it was inside when the brave Americans fought for their very lives against the Mexicans led by Antonio de Santa Anna and his 1800 men.

"The brave Davey Crockett and Jim Bowie led the Americans all but three of whom died in the fighting."

Jupe, who remembered everything he had ever read, and had enjoyed history, muttered, "She's forgetting the actual commander William Travis. But I suppose it is the best she can do."

As the adults and a few small children crowded up in a bunch around the door, their guide stepped back toward the Three Investigators.

"Not joining the others?" she asked.

"Not really if it is just to look into a dark hallway. I've seen actual photographs of the inside. I do have a question," Bob replied. "Wasn't the Alamo a lot smaller and made more from rough stone than this obviously rebuilt and repaired building?"

The girl's eyes went wide. "Uhh-unngh, I really don't know. I just started working here last week. Nobody's said anything about that!"

"Yeah," Pete said now looking curiously at the building. "I saw pictures of the front and that peak wasn't there," he said pointing at the area above the crowded doorway, "and Bob's right. The stones were sort of just set together with some gaps in them, not all nicely mortared together like these are."

She gave them a sad little smile and moved quickly away.

Twenty minutes later the boys hailed another cab but when told he didn't "go just to the stupid station!" the gave up and began walking.

Three blocks on, Jupiter stopped. They were standing on a bridge over an almost invisible river. Down below them was a narrow dirt path that seemed to travel along the river.

"Let's get down there and walk a ways, then maybe we can catch a bus or cab back before the train starts to serve lunch."

The others agreed and they slid and slipped down some dirt to the path fifteen feet below street level.

About what might have been two city blocks away the river split into two forks, but the path only headed to the left. They walked along until that short piece of river petered out and then around until they were moving along the other fork. This only went a few blocks before the river disappeared under a building into a large pipe.

"And, that ends that excitement," Jupe declared. They found a stairway up and were quickly back at street level. "I doubt if walking closer to the station will get any cabbies interested, but there's a bus stop heading the right direction over there. Come on!"

But, before they could get the half block Jupiter spotted one of their Stewards walking in shadows on the other side of the street.

"Look!" he said pulling the others into a shadowy spot and pointing. The man was looking around either trying to find some place—or someone—or to see if he was being followed. "That's kind of suspicious if you ask me."

"Yeah, it is," agreed Pete. "What's the name of this street?"

"Bowie. Figures," Bob said.

"Okay," Jupe said. "He's heading away from the train station and that is that way about four blocks and then to the east another four." He paused trying to decide if it was worth their time, and his exertion, to follow.

Pete tried to make up his mind for him.

"I'm hot and tired and it's really kind of getting muggy around here. You'd think Texas would be all dry but the humidity is not at all nice."

Bob agreed, but Jupe's level of curiosity was twinging.

"Okay. You two head back and see if the train is empty enough for you to do a bit of snooping. I'm going to follow that man at least for a little."

With a promise to try to get a message to them via the Stationmaster in no more than one hour—to tell them he was fine—they split up.

Jupiter Jones noticed everything around him. It was one of the things that made him a great investigator. That, plus the ability to put all sorts of facts together and come up with a good answer as to why things were they way they were.

The Steward headed toward the nearby freeway. He went under it and another two blocks before turning right on Sycamore. It was a short street that curved to the left one block on and the man rounded that corner with Jupe just starting onto Sycamore. There were some old apartment buildings, perhaps six or seven stories tall on his left.

When he arrived at the corner of Sycamore and Heiman there was no sign of the Steward.

Out of frustration he ran to the next intersection and looked up and down that street.

Nothing but cars and a few small children playing on the sidewalks.

But, it was what was directly in front of him that made him groan.

The train depot was right across this new street. In fact, walking toward him from south of the station were Bob and Pete. When they spotted Jupe they stopped and raised their arms in a "what the heck is going on?" manner.

Jupe walked toward them and they met in front of the stone plaza and entry to the depot.

"We thought you were following that guy?" Bob said.

"Yeah."

"So did I," Jupe responded. "He turned one corner and I held back then he turned another and by the time I got there he was just gone! Then, I ran the to the next street… and here I was!"

"But not that Steward?"

"No, Pete. He disappeared. That means he either knew I was following him and raced to get back here or he ducked into one of those apartment building over there." He hooked a thumb over his shoulder pointing at them.

They headed for their train discussing what this might all mean. They came up with no firm idea but were startled by a voice behind them as they neared their platform.

"You young gentlemen giving up on the tourist stuff so early?" It was the polite and cheery voice of the Steward.

Jupiter took a deep breath to steady his voice before replying, "Yes. We saw the Alamo and were not impressed so we though we'd come back here for lunch." He paused and looked carefully at the man's face. "How about you?"

He shrugged. "Took a little walk to stretch my legs. Unless I run up and down the corridors of the train, there's not a lot of chances for exercise on these trips. Well, here we are. See you in the dining car."

With a cheery smile he disappeared in the forward door on one car and the boys in the back door of the next one.

11

A Confession

IT WAS day four—with their final day stop in Houston to come the next morning—and so far the trip had failed to produce any "ghost" experiences except for the one woman, so many of the passengers were starting to complain.

Jupe knew otherwise, but still had no concrete proof that the caped man in black, with no face that could be made out in the darkness of the early mornings—was not supposed to be the ghost. Possibly a killer. When Jupe had tried to follow him, the phantom would turn a corner and seemingly disappear into the next car only to be gone when Jupe got there. Worse yet, the Conductor always seemed to be coming out of his compartment and grabbing Jupe, stopping him from the pursuit.

He was snooping around the car where the Conductor's quarters were located when the man came up behind him.

"You looking for something, kid?" he said looming over the teen.

Jupe gulped but steadied his voice to answer, "Looking for some sort of proof that the man I keep seeing either disappears in one of these rooms, like yours?" he said suggestively. Seeing the man staring at him, he added, "Or at least getting past you and into one of the nearby rooms just when you are coming out. It seems to be too much to be a coincidence, so I'm trying to figure out what's going on."

"Look, son," the Conductor said trying the disguise his impatience, "your poking around into something that is, frankly, not your business, got you nearly lost in the wilderness. Somebody doesn't want you to keep nosing around. I have no idea about that but I certainly don't need the aggravation or the responsibility of keeping tabs on you and those two others. What you claim to have seen just isn't part of this train's repertoire. Our shtick if you will. That means —"

"I know exactly what that means and I don't buy it. This train is nothing but an extended amusement park ride with a ghost theme, and it isn't all that believable."

The man before him drew himself up to his full height and sighed heavily.

"Okay," he said sounding defeated. "I'm going to do something I shouldn't but I think you need to know a few things in order to keep you safe and not snooping. Can I trust you to keep the company's secret?" He looked meaningfully at Jupe.

"Even from my two associates?"

The Conductor closed his eyes and pinched the bridge of his nose between his right thumb and forefinger. "Okay," he said. "Fine. But, only them! Nobody else. Understand?" Jupe nodded. "Okay, come to the front of the train with me. I have something you need to see."

They headed forward until they reached the final "public" car. At the front end was a bar across the last few feet before the door to the next car. The Conductor took out a set of keys and inserted one in the lock on the bar. It clicked open and he swung it up and away before stepping forward to the door. It also was locked as was the one on the other side of the open area between cars.

There was no protective cowling so Jupe could see the tracks below and the sky above as he stepped across.

In a moment he and Jupe were standing inside the corridor running the length of the "secret" car.

The man gave him a smile that sent a chill down Jupiter's spine.

"Think you're ready to know the truth?"

Jupiter Jones gulped but nodded.

"Right!" With that the man opened the first of two doors in the car and made a sweeping motion inviting Jupe to step inside.

"Golly!" Jupe exclaimed as he did and could see what the car held.

"Where the heck can he have gotten to?" Pete asked causing Bob to shrug.

"Don't know. Unless he got tossed off the train he has to be somewhere. Right?"

"I don't think Jupe would fall for the same trick twice, but if he did we need to find out if he's on the train or not and then tell someone."

They set off from car nine where they had been standing to search as far to the rear as they could. Carefully to not make any noise they tried each compartment's door handle. Every compartment in this first car was firmly locked which they expected since a good number of passengers would be in the dining car for the first dinner sitting while many others would be in the observation car watching the scenery pass by. They retraced their steps and moved past their room.

The next car back had the same twelve locked doors.

But, and to both their surprises, the very last compartment's door handle in the car just in front of the dining car, turned. Both boys froze hoping against hope that there was nobody inside.

Bob whose hand was on the handle, pushed the door to the

side an inch. He pressed his right eye to the gap and let out a sigh of relief. He slid the door all the way into the wall.

"It's empty, Pete," he proclaimed. "Come on in."

Once they were both inside, he closed the door and turned on the lights.

"Will you take a look at that!" Pete exclaimed.

Sitting on the top of the one visible bunk was an old cigar box, open, and in that box were three packets of money. The top bills all seemed to be fifty or one hundred dollar denominations. But that wasn't what really caught their eyes.

That honor was given to the four brick-sized bundles of plastic-wrapped, green marijuana. The boys recognized it from a video their teacher had shown in conjunction with their school's Be Friends With a Cop day the previous April.

"We have to get out of there and find Jupe and tell him," Bob stated.

"We have to get out of here and either tell a policeman in the next town we stop at, or just get out and keep out mouths shut!"

"Let's find Jupe. He'll know what to do!"

The Conductor closed the only door to the corridor and pulled over a chair without sitting down.

The boy stepped cautiously to one side turning quickly in case this were a trick and the man was going to attack him. But the Conductor turned on a light switch before taking a seat and looking at Jupe.

"So, yes, this is where the magic happens," he said pointing over Jupe's shoulder. When the teen turned his head and caught sight of what ran nearly the entire length of the wall, his body whipped around at what he saw.

"Computers and a ton of monitors?" he hoarsely whispered.

"That, son, is some state of the art computer set-up that controls our ghosts," the Conductor replied. "About the best the company could afford. You see, this entire train is, as you pointed out, an amusement park ride of sorts filled with ghosts. And, yeah, each car has its own one. Comes out of a small compartment right next to the inter-car door and runs on thin cables up and down the corridor. Everything is operated from this car, this room, and all on a predetermined schedule. Just like Disneyland and a lot of amusement parks, we have a set schedule for everything that happens in and outside the train, and only the Chief Engineer and I can make any changes. And," he said with a shake of his head, "we do not make changes!" He looked meaningfully at Jupe.

"This computer can send sounds into each car long enough to get some folk out of their rooms in time to see the ghost disappear to one end or the other, depending on what these monitors show where people are. Then it's back into a small compartment and the door snaps shut before anyone can get to the corner to see the magic." He grinned. Sometimes we get people crowded at one end only to have the ghost from the other end sneak up on then and scream its little head off!"

He sounded a bit weary as he described some of the equipment before suggesting Jupe might want to see a personal demonstration of the train's "ghosts."

"I've seen it several times and you've stopped me from following him, or it. That's suspicious you have to admit."

"No, I don't and I say that because we haven't turned the ghosts on yet. That starts tonight. So far we've played with lights and added a few sounds to the audio system in the cars, but no ghost. Other than the misbehaving one that scared that woman. Come on; I'll show it to you." Donlevy picked up what looked like a remote control.

He stopped out in the corridor and turned to Jupe. Just so you know, the reason I am in the corridor when you charge through is because I am usually taking a break from my paperwork. That compartment is my office. The office of whoever is the Conductor. And, I was not supposed to make this run. I did the NOLa to La-La Land run last week and was supposed to have this run off, but the regular man had an accident on the way to the station and was laid up in the hospital for a couple days. He'll make the return trip and I get to go back as a passenger."

"Can I ask a question?"

"Sure, kid," Donlevy sighed. "Ask away."

"Okay, it's just that all those computers and monitors look sort of impressive, but it's kind of old. Couldn't a couple Apple or IBM desktop computers do everything?"

Donlevy laughed and patted Jupe in the shoulder. "Yeah. It's practically ancient and yet only four years ago it was new. This all will be replace in about a year with just one small computer that will run from the Conductor's office. This car will be retired and another passenger car will take its place."

They left the compartment and headed back into the front public sleeper car.

"Stand right there," the Conductor told the Investigator. "And watch the corner." With that he opened a hidden door in the wall facing the doorway. Then, after checking that nobody was coming down the corridor he flipped a switch and pressed several buttons on his remote. The ceiling lights went out, dim green lights came on at floor level, and the shades over the corridor windows closed and a little CO_2 "fog" drifted down.

All of a sudden, a ghostly glow came from the far end of the car accompanied by some rather spooky noises. In seconds Jupe felt every hair on the back of his neck stand straight out as a ghost slid around the corner. It brushed past him before taking a sharp turn to the left and disappearing in the wall. Outside the side door a green light flickered and wavered swiftly rising up until it was no longer visible.

"And that," the Conductor told him, "is our ghost. He does not, by the way, go through the wall there. There is a small hatch that opens in the darkened recesses and the rig slips inside before snapping shut. So far it has been before anyone could turn the corner."

"Except for that woman, Jupe stated.

"Yeah, except for that."

Now recovered from his surprise and very curious about how the illusion operated, Jupe questioned the man on how it all worked.

"If you notice our ceilings are very dark and the lights actually stick down four inches. That leaves very dark shadows that hide a series of very small wires—our track if you will. The ghost is nothing more that a thin silvery silk sheet with a few hoops and other things to give it some shape, and a series of tiny pulsating lights that give it the ghostly appearance. Those get power from the overhead wires in case you are interested."

"But, the ghost or whatever I saw was definitely not dangling from wires. It wore dark shoes. And I could hear the footsteps as it ran away from me."

The Conductor laughed. "Well then, it could have been any one of the crew or about half the male passengers on this train. We all wear black shoes!"

Yes, Jupe thought, you all do.

But only the Conductor wore black Oxford loafers...

...and so did the mysterious phantom *in the hallway!*

12

One Unscheduled Body in an Unlikely Place

IT HAD been Bob suggesting they ought to do some quiet exploration of the train and the unlocked compartment late that night. Jupe agreed but Pete was feeling exhausted and asked to be left in the compartment.

"Do you think he's getting sick?" Bob asked.

"Nope." Jupe sounded definite. "I think Pete has been worrying about so many little things—I hear him fidgeting in his bunk every night—that he really has exhausted himself. We'll need all hands at some point so we'll give him the night off."

During the previous nights Jupe had stayed awake as much as he could to see if there was a pattern to the various train personnel and when they disappeared for the night. Obviously he'd fallen asleep but had been up around one in the morning when no sounds—other that the phantom that first night—could be heard.

Now, as that time approached, he and Bob stepped into the corridor and shut the door behind them being as quiet as possible. They checked the five cars forward of their own seeing or hearing nothing.

Bob pointed to the back of the train then the front with a questioning look in his eyes. Jupe thought about it and pointed to the front. They were only a couple cars from the dining car where the Stewards might still be at work.

They passed between their car and the one where the Conductor had intercepted Jupe with no incidents. Even as they crossed through the accordion gap to the next car all seemed well.

But it was Bob and his sensitive nose that stopped them as they passed the last compartment before heading forward again.

"What's that stench?" he said trying to whisper around his fingers that were clenching his nose.

"That," Jupe said with more than a hint of dismay, "is not a healthy smell. The junkyard gets that when something crawls under something else and gets trapped."

Bob gulped as the message came through as clearly as the bad smell. "This is where Pete and I found the money and the drugs."

There was something no longer alive in this car, and they both realized it must be from the compartment they were in front of.

"We should go tell someone," Bob determined.

Jupe shook his head and grabbed the handle of the door giving it a test twist. He was honestly surprised when it turned and the door opened a crack. But, this also allowed even more of the horrific smell to escape and they both began gagging.

They closed the door and retreated to the small drinking fountain in the middle of the car where they soaked their handkerchiefs and tied them over their mouths and noses.

It did little to disguise the smell but made them feel better.

Jupe, the bravest—or most foolhardy according to both Bob and Pete—stepped inside and quickly walked over to the window which he unlatched and shoved upward.

Bob came in closing the door and was happy to find a lot of the smell was dissipating in the wind that entered from outside.

It was only then Jupe went back to the door and turned the overhead light on.

Both stared. The room was empty!

At least there was no visible body... or dead animal—which is what Bob was praying would be the source of the smell. He pointed to the mattress where there was no reappearance of either the money box or anything else.

Taking a breath to steady his nerves, Jupe slid the bathroom door open. There was nothing inside the tiny cubicle either.

Jupe was about to admit he was stumped. Something *had* been inside the compartment and it had been dead and even decomposing, which was a smell they recognized. He looked around the room. It was one of the ones with a trio of bunks like their own. The upper berths were still folded up and away but the lower one was down and flat, although it was unmade.

"This must be one of the three unsold rooms," he whispered to his friend. "But, if that's right, then why is the sofa folded down?"

"I honestly don't want to know, Jupe. I'm just not that curious. Can we just go back to our room and forget about this? Let someone in charge find this stinky room?"

"No." It was a flat and definite answer, the one Bob had not wished to hear.

Jupe reached out and took hold of the front of the lower bunk and lifted it up.

The smell that hit them, even with their makeshift masks and the constant breeze from outside, made them rush to the window where they both threw up. Jupe hoped it would not stick to the side of the train as he pulled his head back inside.

The body was dressed in a type of coverall they had seen in Los Angeles and again in the El Paso station on a few of the luggage handlers. But, the state of decomposition told them both this person—man?— had been dead far longer than the full day and night since that stop.

"How do you think he died? A heart attack, maybe?"

Jupe looked down and shook his head. "Murdered, Records. That knife in the gut area isn't there because someone set it down to perform CPR. And, I'd say at least since we left Los Angeles. Maybe even a day before." He was about to close the top when he spotted a bundle of something about football size, wrapped in dark paper and plastic wrap sitting near the corpse's knees.

He closed his eyes and reached in, picking the package up from its resting place along the dead body's left side using just his fingertips on one loose end.

"Come on, and let's get out of there," he said to Bob as he stuck the package under his shirt.

A fast look up and down the hall showed nobody coming so they scooted out and back toward their own car and safety of their compartment.

They knew they were trailing the same terrible smell from the room so they went past their own room and a full car farther to the rear of the train before backtracking and entering their compartment.

The smell woke Pete who sat bolt upright and gagged.

"Quick. Get out of these clothes and we'll get them shoved into the garbage bags we packed for dirty clothes."

While they did this, Pete slipped down to the floor and opened their window a little. Three minutes later the clothes were tied tightly in the plastic and the room had pretty much cleared of the smell.

"Now, let's see what was in that storage area worth someone being killed over," Jupe stated. Pete stared as if he'd seen a real ghost but said nothing as the lead member of their team peeled back more than ten layers of plastic wrap at one end along with five layers of brown, butchers' paper.

"Well," he said slowly. "That explains that." He slid out some papers that were all bundled together. Inside the now visible end of the package were twenty stacks of one hundred dollar bills.

He carefully examined a few of the bills from the one bundle he'd extracted. He spread out about a dozen of the bills on his bunk.

"Someone is doing something very bad and using this train to help transport these," Jupiter said tapping the closest bill. "If you will both notice, all these bills have the same serial number. Fellows, we've stumbled on a really good mystery with counterfeit money, drugs and a murder, and now we need to find out who is the forger or at least their delivery person!"

Pete gulped.

Bob said ominously, "Unless that body we found was the delivery man. If it was, them we probably have the murderer on this train!"

Pete gulped again, this time making a loud noise.

13
Attacked!

AT BREAKFAST that morning nothing was being said about the discovery of any body or any smell. In fact, Jupe noticed when they stepped from their compartment that there was a distinct smell of some sort of disinfectant spray and over the top of that was something else smelling slightly of wild flowers.

"Someone found our friend and got rid of him, then they sprayed everything to get rid of the odor," Jupe told Pete and Bob as they entered the dining car. "Or knows the person who found out somebody had been in there and took that bundle. I'll bet whoever killed that man is furious right about now."

The Steward, the man who both provided the cocoa and espresso drinks as well as the one they spotted in El Paso and San Antonio, came to their table causing them to stop talking about anything.

"Normal breakfast for my fine, young friends?" His voice sounded a bit strained as if he was under some emotional pressure.

On a whim, Jupiter decided to try to get some information from the man. "I'm a bit tired so the coffee and cocoa will be great, but I woke up to some horrible smell around, oh, I don't know, but perhaps two or three. Took away my appetite! Did you catch a whiff of it?"

The man stood, looking as if he were pondering the question. "Nope. Slept like a log until 5:30. Might have been us passing a place to the west of Houston where they burn rubbish twenty-four hours a day. Sometimes they also burn all the road kill the state police scoop up. Might have been that."

"Yeah," Jupe responded slowly, "might have been... but back to ordering. I'll have the waffles and corned beef hash with two over easy eggs on top."

"Because you're not so hungry?" The Steward had a smirk on his face.

Jupe shrugged. "The smell is gone so, yeah, I'm hungry, again."

Bob and Pete both felt very little hunger from the memory of the smells of death or even the knowledge of it, so they ordered the cocoa drink plus orange juice for Bob and grapefruit juice for Pete.

"I'll bring you some toast in case you feel like a nibble," the man said giving them a rather forced smile.

The train pulled into Houston's station at 10:00 AM and would remain there according to the schedule until midnight. Then it would be a forty-hour ride to New Orleans with two stops of just five minutes each to pick up mail sacks—one of them, Schriever, Louisiana, would be at midnight before pulling into their final destination so no announcement would be made over the public address system.

The Investigators ate in near silence. Watching Jupe wolf down his food made the other two even less hungry and they soon pushed their cups and glasses away.

"What are we gonna do in Houston?" Pete asked.

"I hope it isn't just hanging around the station to see if the Steward makes another walking trip," Bob stated under his breath.

The boys decided to get off the train and check the guide rack in the station.

The platform for the Houston station was about as long as the entire train. Inside, they perused several of the offerings deciding on the Museum of Natural Science as the sort of place they could really enjoy. This was made more so by a note in one guide that it was currently hosting an "exhibit of crimes and criminal investigation techniques in the modern era."

Outside the station they spotted the bus area and went to find one heading south that would get them close. To Bob's surprise, right in front of the queue was one with NAT'L SCI MUSEUM on the front.

They dropped their quarters in the slot and accepted transfer strips just in case they needed them.

The exhibits at the museum would be enough to fill their entire stop. There was a glass-covered butterfly area they could walk through, a planetarium, and even a theater showing nature movie shorts every twenty minutes.

After entering the main building, they attached themselves to the free tour group just leaving the entry. It was meant to interest people in various areas and then to release them after just thirty minutes. All three of the Investigators were quiet and listened as she described the areas covering flight and rockets, power generation, and even the study of old bones, or "anthropology" as she termed it.

Their ears perked up at the limited time area regarding Crime Detection.

In fact, they hung back as the group left to the next room— modern farming and agriculture—so they could spend the maximum time in the "crime" room.

There were about fifty small displays, each with a poster describing that aspect in fair detail. They spent nearly an hour looking through things having to do with unsolved murders and kidnappings of famous people. But their leader suddenly stood up straight.

Pointing to their right, Jupe whispered, "Look!"

The other two turned to see what their friend meant.

Counterfeiting Through the Ages said the banner over a twenty-foot-long glass-enclosed display case. Inside were items like some hand-stamped phony coins from a period of more that two hundred years, a small but very complete printing press, examples of the sort of printing plates counterfeiters used and a special area with more than three dozen actual counterfeit bills ranging from fives to hundreds and even a five hundred dollar bill that Jupe took a look at and snorted.

"That one would have been easy to spot," he declared.

"Why?" Bob and Pete chorused taking a close look but seeing nothing to earmark that bill.

Jupe sighed heavily. "Who is on the five hundred dollar bill?"

The others shrugged having never seen one nor studied disused or infrequently used legal tender.

"Well, it sure the heck isn't Franklin Roosevelt! It was President McKinley. And, to top things off they stopped printing them at the end of the Second World War, not 1949 like that one says was its printing series date."

"That boy knows a lot about counterfeit money," a man behind them was saying to his wife. He seemed impressed.

"Well, I think it is a sin that little children should know about something illegal," she replied with a sniff.

Jupe turned around slowly to face the woman. "And just how, pray tell, should we *little children* go about spotting illegal things and not fall prey to them unless we study them? Please answer that, ma'am or have your husband do it if it is beyond your *little woman's* mind! Come on, fellows. Let's get away from the narrow-minded old lady."

They moved away as a team and were already in the next

room before the woman found her voice and demanded they come back and apologize.

They kept moving and soon left the museum.

There was a large park area in front of and around the museum so they walked through it stopping at a hot dog cart to have an early lunch before deciding to walk back to the train depot.

They passed by the large Museum of Fine Arts and several undeveloped plots interspersed with housing and business buildings.

It was about the time they crossed under a freeway on a street named Milan that Jupe stopped.

"I've had enough fun walking. The joy has all but disappeared from my heart. Let's find a bus stop and ride back," he stated. The others agreed and a block later they arrived at a stop with a bus just pulling away.

Jupe started running forward arms flapping and was about to give up when the bus stopped and the side door opened.

They got inside, with Jupe slightly out of breath, a half minute later only to find it was the wrong bus.

"But the right one'll be along in about two minutes. Here," the driver offered tearing off three transfer strips. "Use those and you wont have to pay again!"

The next bus was the one they wanted and the driver barely looked at their transfers.

Some twenty blocks later they arrived at the train station and wearily climbed aboard.

It was too late for lunch service but they wandered to the dining car. There, the Steward they'd spotted before and the woman chef were sitting having coffee.

"Look at what the cat dragged in, girl," the man stated

smiling and pointing at the boys.

She slapped the Steward on his forearm. "You go get these tired-lookin' boys some colas while I make them some sandwiches." Looking right at Jupe, she asked, "You are hungry, aren't you?"

They nodded and nine minutes later gratefully accepted some grilled tunafish sandwiches with cole slaw and dill pickle spears.

They ate another full meal at the dinner seating and moved to the observation car until it turned nine. There were still three hours before the train would pull out of Houston Station remaining, and the sun was nearly down as the trio headed to their compartment and their bunks.

Bob, still restless from the day in Houston, tossed and turned for hours until he finally gave up, lowered himself to the floor and got dressed.

I can spend a better time in the observation car, he thought. The door opened with only a slight rise in the noise, and two snores told him the others were still asleep.

He walked through the wobbling car to the back end, slid the door between his car and the open area to the side and stepped to the next car.

The next door refused to open and the one he'd come through snapped shut behind him.

He tried again to open the next car but the handle would not turn. He turned around feeling the draft from the incomplete seal of the wide rubber gaskets and tried the handle of their car.

It also refused to budge.

Bob felt a small bit of panic seeping into his mind. He wasn't dressed to be outside with the wind whipping around and was starting to feel slightly cold.

Again he tried to open both doors and still had no success. He might have tried pounding on one or both, but at this hour there would be nobody to hear him.

Every minute or so he tried both locks. His fingers were getting tired and he was about at the point he was going to pound away when his ears picked up a click that he couldn't associate with the tracks zipping past below him.

He tried the lock on their car... nothing. He tried the lock on the next car back and it almost magically moved. His thumb pressed harder and it finally engaged. He was able to pull to door to the side and slip through.

Bob slumped to the floor trying to warm up and also to stop shivering which was not so much from the cold as it was from the panic he'd finally given into.

He sat there five minutes before standing up. Without thinking that he had to cross two more gaps, he reached the other end of this car and opened the door.

At the last possible second his brain engaged and he shoved his foot back in time to stop the open door from fully closing. But, he needn't have bothered because the next car's door opened with ease as did the one between that and the dining car.

He passed the young woman chef as she was sitting at a table reading a romance novel, the sort with the long-haired man with an open shirt holding a fainting "maiden" in his strong arms.

She looked up only long enough to smile at him and nod before going back to her reading.

He continued between tables and to the final door. Both sides, again, opened without any resistance.

Standing on the lower floor of the observation car he

looked down the gloomy walkway between the rows of seats. He felt a little shiver running down his back but ignored it.

Bob turned to the left and started up the very dark spiral stairs, but he got no further than the seventh step when something grabbed his right shoulder, yanking him sharply back and down. Before he might have crashed to the floor something hit him on the back of the head.

The last thing he remembered thinking was, "You really *do* see stars..." as darkness enveloped him totally.

There was sunshine coming into the car when he woke up. It was not without help as a Steward, their favorite mystery man, splashed a glass of water in his face.

"I was making the morning rounds picking up glasses and stuff when I found you. You slip on the stairs in the dark? They're kinda dangerous which is why I keep telling the Conductor we ought to lock this car up after midnight. You okay?"

The Investigator gently rubbed at the rather large knot on the back of his head.

"I got hit by someone," he stated.

"Don't ya think you might have fallen and it just felt like you got hit?"

Bob slowly shook his head. It made it hurt more. "No. It was someone grabbing my arm, pulling me back and hitting me. Definitely in that order. We need to tell the Conductor or someone."

"Well, if we do that the law says we got to stop the train and investigate that. Didn't I hear one of you three boys you have a job to get home to?"

Bob groaned. He was already about to be a day late; he could possibly talk himself out of dismissal for that, but two days? That made his head hurt even more.

He headed back toward the front of the train. The Steward called out after him as he opened the sliding door, "Your friends haven't come to breakfast yet, and it's a little early, but my bet is the cook might make you a stack of pancakes or something."

Bob shook his head—another bad decision—saying, "I don't have the appetite for anything. I've been clobbered, but if I report it everyone is going to hate me. I'm going back to bed!"

14
The Intrusion

ONE HOUR after breakfast the boys went on the official tour of the rear engine. It was Donlevy the Conductor who gathered a group of about twenty interested people in the observation car.

"If everyone could settle down," he called out to the murmuring crowd. "I say, settle down back there, please!" The people turned to face his voice and their comments and conversation faded away over the next fifteen seconds.

Donlevy had to make one more plea to a woman who just kept up a constant conversation with the man—her husband? —standing next to her trying to look like he didn't know who she was.

"Madam, please! If you want to talk, kindly do so in another car or this one once the rest of use leave. Thank you!"

She huffed and muttered something Bob caught sounding like, "What a nerve!" He thought she should be telling herself that, but she did stop talking.

"Fine. Now, we are about to enter the private sleeping car for this train's personnel before we get to the rear locomotive. Kindly make as little noise as possible so as not to disturb people who have been up all night making sure this train runs smoothly. We have shut this locomotive's engine down so you will be able to hear me once we are inside."

The group followed him through the locked door and down the passageway.

The talkative woman commented in a voice that could have been heard from the back of any auditorium, "It is certainly hot in here. I hope that man doesn't expect us to remain for more than a few seconds!" Her husband hushed her leading to a, "Well, I never!" from her but glares from those nearest to her shut her up.

Inside the locomotive, and once people settled down, the Conductor stood on top of one of the engine halves and began his tour speech.

To Jupe it sounded like the canned tour at Universal Studios where college kids recited the same spiel over and over and over again until their heads exploded and they went back to school. Inside his head he was hearing:

"One the left side of the tram is the harbor outside the small New England fishing village where both Jessica Fletcher wrote and solved all those murder mysteries and if you are old enough to remember it is also the South Pacific island where McHale's Navy called home... and also where the dreaded shark, Jaws first appeared and... oh my god!... look over to the right... It's the shark of all sharks... Keep your arms and heads inside the tram while I get out my gun." **Pop pop pop**. *"Well that's got him and we're all safe... and we're moving again so keep those arms inside and please do not let children toss things into the lagoon........... and as we go up and around the hill you will see the famous Frankenstein's Arch where the dreaded monster first appeared lit by lightning ...."*

What the Conductor was telling the crowd was mostly what the Three Investigators had heard from the Engineer with a bit of marketing speak added to try to make the haunting and the dead bodies seem to be at the very heart of why people ought to be frightened when they spotted one of the ghosts... now more than likely to be that evening.

"One of the skeletons was still in a hammock... the one you

see behind me! They could come to visit and haunt the train this very night," he said ominously.

Bingo! thought the investigator.

"It is generally around Houston on the eastward run and about Phoenix on the western direction we see them! I guess they get tired of long train trips and get a little cranky—Ha-ha-ha!"

"Oh, brother," Jupe said so low that only Pete caught it. The First Investigator raised his hand.

"Yes? A question from one of our young passengers?"

"The smell of all the diesel is making me queasy. Would it be okay if we went back to our room?"

The man dithered a moment before nodding. "Please be as quiet as you can on your way though the private car and move to the rest of the train smartly!"

Jupe led Bob and Pete out of the locomotive and down the passageway. Once they reached the observation car, Bob grabbed Jupe's shoulder and stopped the teen. "What was all that about?"

"I only wanted the rest of the crew to see that we had left on the tour. Now that the Conductor is busy we should be able to get to the front of the train and see if there is anything we might investigate."

"Oh," came from his two companions.

As they passed through the dining car Jupe noticed the absence of any Stewards. Not even the chef was visible. They headed through the first two cars with berthing compartments and into their own.

Jupe stopped suddenly.

Bob and Pete ran into his back but didn't say anything.

They could all see the door to their room was open and

there were sounds of someone rifling through their belongings.

Motioning Bob to get down on his hands and knees—which made the tall boy stare questioningly at Jupe, but he did it, Jupiter stepped into the open door and demanded, "What the heck are you doing in here?"

It surprised him all the more to see *not* their normal room attendant, but the dining Steward, Joseph Miller, and he had his right hand under Bob's mattress where he had been digging around.

The man's eyes went wide as saucers and he took a step toward Jupe, but stopped and a grin came to his face.

"Just helping the Porters, my little man. One of them is really sick and they're shorthanded, so a couple of us Stewards are giving them a hand making beds and stuff. I was just about to tuck everything in…" and he looked at the other two bunks that had obviously been searched and were in great disarray.

"So, uhh, I'll just make these bunks and then get out of here," he finished turning away from Jupe.

Jupe motioned Bob to rise and the three of them stood in the doorway with Bob even with the back of the door, Jupe in the middle blocking the way out, and Pete at the front in case the man tried to slip past them.

But, he didn't. He did straighten the bunks and made their beds before leaving. "If you need clean towels just ring. Either a Porter or one of us Stewards will bring you some. Bye."

What added to their suspicion he had been searching, not straightening, the room was the fact he disappeared into the next car back even though there were other compartments in this one he might have also "cleaned."

With their door finally closed, Jupe let out a deep breath he'd been holding. "At least we know he couldn't have found that package," he said.

It was true. He and Bob and made a two-man tower and the taller boy had shoved the package into a handy vent just above and outside their compartment earlier. Unless you knew where to look, it was invisible to anyone standing in the corridor.

"Do we report him to the Conductor?" Pete wanted to know.

"We should," Bob added.

"Okay, then we will, if you insist. But I still have my doubts about the Conductor. I can't believe it is coincidence he has stopped us more than once when we've spotted the man in black and he just happens to be in the passageway of the next car in time to miss the man and catch us!" Jupe was looking angry at the moment so the other two decided to not push the matter.

The boys stayed in their compartment until lunch time just to ensure the Steward had no further opportunity to continue his fruitless search.

That man avoided them in the dining car where they were served by another of the Stewards, the youngest of the crew.

"Isn't this Joseph's table?" Jupe asked putting on his best innocent voice and look.

The young man looked around and leaned down so only the boys might hear him. "Yeah, but Joseph says he don't want to do this table today. Says I gotta, so I guess I gotta."

He set down their plates with turkey sandwiches, carrot sticks and a small fruit cup before straightening up. "Sorry if I don't satisfy," he told them before moving on.

"Now," Jupe declared around a large bite of his sandwich,

"I think we have to talk to the Conductor. I don't like the idea that our regular Steward was found in our room, practically ransacking it, and then he changes tables all of a sudden. It isn't right."

The three boys decided to look up the man after they ate.

They went back to check their compartment. It had not been opened which they knew because the single hair Jupe had placed, using a bit of his own saliva, between the door edge and the jamb, was still there. So, they headed forward. Nowhere along the way to the locked front car did they see a sign of the man.

"He might be inside the front car," Bob offered.

"Yes, Jupe answered, "but he also could be at the back of the train either in the observation car or their private sleeper. I don't want us to divide up so let's head back again."

The found the Conductor sitting in one of the swivel seats in the observation car's main floor. He appeared to be listening to something, but sported no headphones. Sensing he was being looked at he opened first his right then his left eye.

"Well, well, well, if it isn't the carsick trio? What brings you back out into the public, boys?"

Jupe sat down on the seat next to him and used the Conductor's own left leg to swing him around to face him.

"Listen. We are not little boys and we have a very serious complaint that you need to take to heart. Our room was ransacked. What they call in spy movies, 'tossed,' and we caught the person doing it!"

He now had the Conductor's full attention. "Yes," he agreed, "that is most serious. Do you know the passenger's name?"

Jupe, Bob and Pete all shook their heads and the Conductor

looked at them all now worried at what he was going to hear. Then, his face changed and he smiled. "It isn't that mystery man in black you claim to have seen, is it?"

Jupe's face scowled. "No. It was one of this train's Stewards, Joseph Miller, and he was tearing our room apart when we headed back from your tour. He had an excuse that he was helping one of the Porters, but he wasn't making our bunks until we caught him."

They told the Conductor about the strange way the man acted and also how he's switched tables at lunch so he did not have to look at the three of them.

Seeing how Donlevy was honestly take aback by this turn of events, Jupe decided they would further take him into their confidence.

"Mr Donlevy. Would you say you are an honest man?"

"Of course I am," he stated uncategorically. "Who's said different?"

"Nobody so far..."

Jupe and Bob and Pete then told him about the dead body that was there stinking to high heaven before it disappeared and no trace of the bad odor remained, and the package of counterfeit money, and how they had spotted Miller in town at least in El Paso and San Antonio.

They detailed their violent attack shortly after seeing the man at their first stop and how at the second stop he'd led them on a round-about trip right back to the train station.

By the time they finished Donlevy was white with both anger and fear.

"I'll get to the bottom of this!" he promised before launching himself up and out of his seat.

15

Bob and Pete Both Encounter *That Man*

LATE THAT evening as they were talking in whispers across the gap between their bunks, Bob and Pete stopped. They had both heard the noise coming from over their heads. It certainly wasn't Jupe as he was snoring merrily away below them.

"W-w-was that ...footsteps?" Pete stammered out.

Bob could only nod and they both looked at the ceiling of the compartment. Every second or so a creaking noise came from above them along with a *thunk*. Whoever was up there —or *whatever* it was!—must have been fighting terrific headwinds to be able to move around without falling off the train.

The steps were traveling from the forward part of their car heading back. But, a moment later they stopped. Suddenly they heard a heavy thump as if whoever was up there had fallen, or possibly jumped the gap to the next car back. Whatever it had been, the sounds stopped.

The two boys were both white with fright as they finally looked across the short gap at each other.

Jupiter continued to sleep soundly and giving out his usual cacophony of snores and snorts.

Bob pointed to the door and gave a questioning look to Pete. For his part, Pete had tried to push himself back almost to the wall so he might become invisible. His covers were pulled up to his nose, and Bob could tell he was shivering.

"What so we do?" Bob hissed. Then, a sudden notion came into his mind. *Had they locked their compartment door?* That sent an icy chill up and down his spine a couple times. "The door?" he hissed again.

Pete shrugged. "I don't know. I don't remember. Who was last inside?"

They both knew it had been Bob as Jupe generally went headlong into whatever there might be before the others could try to get ahead of him. That included their compartment.

"Do you want to check it?" Bob asked.

Pete shook his head. "Nopc!"

Bob took a deep breath and let himself down to the floor as quietly as he could. He took the five steps to the door and looked at the lock in the darkness. "I can't tell. It's too dark," he hissed.

"Did you try feeling it?"

"Oh." Bob felt a little foolish as he reached out and ran his fingers over the lock trying to recall if pointing out to the side meant it was locked, or if straight up was. He mentally shrugged and started to turn the handle. When it stopped just a few degrees around he heaved a great sigh of relief.

"It's been locked. Now what do we do?"

"I don't know!" came back the hissed response.

"Fine!" But Bob felt the situation was anything *but* fine and so he reached back for the handle and tried it again. It still refused to turn so he twisted the lock.

"What are you doing?" came Pete's slightly desperate voice as he began getting out from under his covers. He quickly climbed down and was standing next to Bob before the taller boy opened the door.

It slid mostly quietly into the wall and they both tried to step into the corridor at the same time. After a few seconds of jostling around Pete slipped into the hall first followed closely by Bob.

It was then the door to the outside at the back of their car opened and a hard gust of cold wind blew into the two boys.

But that wasn't what send ice down their spines and froze them to the spot! It was the fact that, exactly as Jupe had reported, the door had been opened just long enough for the mystery man dressed in black to climb in. He slammed the door behind him and turned their direction.

This time it was Bob who got back through the compartment door as he practically shoved Pete to the floor.

Poor Pete was still getting to his feet when the man took a few steps toward them. He looked up and into the shadow covering the man-in-black's face.

For his part, the mystery man seemed genuinely shocked to find one of the passengers sitting in the passage. He let out a startled grunt before he took several steps forward causing Pete to scoot back and into the boys' room on his rump.

The man stepped up to the door and in a very harsh whisper warned, "Try to follow me and you'll all die!" Then, he turned and ran toward the front of the train, *the way he'd come outside their car!* The sounds of the interconnecting door opening and closing said he had left their car.

Bob noticed that Pete wasn't moving so he tapped his friend on the shoulder.

"Eeepp!" squeaked Pete.

"Will you two please shut up?" Jupe's weary voice came from where it was buried in his pillow.

"Jupe!" Bob's said in a strained but normal volume of voice. "It was *that* man! In all black! He just said he'd kill us."

In two-seconds Jupe was out of his low bunk and standing with his fellow investigators. He reached past the stunned Bob and flicked the light switch up. The lights in the compartment came on blinding all three boys for a few seconds.

Pete, with Jupe's help, got to his feet. He was panting from the scare he and Bob had just had. Although Pete was nearly paralyzed from fright, Jupe went into action. Seconds later he had his trousers on and was pulling on his Polo-style shirt.

"You two can stay or come, but I'm going after whoever that is!"

Both Pete and Bob decided that staying behind was the best course of action so Jupe stepped past them and headed forward. He reached the cross-over and soon had entered the next car.

Not at all to his surprise, the Conductor was standing in the corridor blocking him from moving any farther forward than the car in front of theirs.

"You? Again? I've told you to stop making noise at night, haven't I?"

In a very calm voice, Jupe stated, "If anybody is making noise, sir, it is you. And I assure you that if you consider things rationally you will realize I *just* entered this car while you were disturbed probably a minute earlier. Long enough, certainly, to get dressed… unless you were already in those dark trousers?"

The man narrowed his eyes and looked at Jupe. If he believed the teen would blink first, he totally underestimated his adversary. Jupe had practiced his non-blinking stare and could keep it up for nearly a minute. Most adults gave up in about half that time. Within thirty-six seconds his eyes were starting to water but the Conductor not only blinked but turned his face away from Jupiter.

"Okay. Listen," the man said turning back and blinking several times. "I've had two other reports of this strange figure all dressed in black in the last two days from other passengers. That plus one of my Porters says he heard one of you kids... or, I mean one of you *young men* got hit over the head in the observation car the other morning."

Jupe nodded but kept his mouth shut figuring the older man would feel uncomfortable enough with the silence and start speaking again. He only had to wait a quarter minute.

"So, I'm ready to talk if you can tell me what you've seen and heard and when that was."

He pointed to the back of the train and he and Jupe headed for the observation car.

On the way through the dining car Jupe believe he caught a glimpse of one of the train personnel lurking inside the small kitchen... and it wasn't the pretty chef!

16
Missing!

WHILE HOUSTON had been a bit more interesting than their other two stops, it could not overcome the boredom that was seeping into all the passengers as they traversed the rest of the wide state of Texas and headed toward their destination nearly another full day away.

So far, only about fifteen people had stated they had witnessed the "ghosts" of the train as they flew up and down their cars' corridor. Everyone else was questioning if the tickets had been worth what they'd paid.

The extra day of delays was not helping in the least. Bob was feeling it the most as he just knew his job would have disappeared before he managed to get to a phone in New Orleans. The one radio phone on the train was not for use by the passengers and even for the crew it was an Emergency Only phone.

Making matters worse, Bob forgot to make a call when they had access to a pay phone in Houston.

What did help was that the Engineer declared the final two days of meals and non-alcoholic drinks were "on the company." He told them all the owners felt bad about the unavoidable extra travel time and they were doing everything they could to reschedule everybody's plane trips back out to Los Angeles. This announcement came during lunch that day after they left Houston.

Jupe said out loud that he wondered why their stops were all in Texas and not spread out more, but neither Bob nor Pete had a response.

"If it were up to me I'd have stopped in Tucson, San

Antonio and Houston but not El Paso!"

Nobody was paying Jupe a lot of attention at the moment so he shrugged and went back to studying the route map.

Five minutes later he also wondered out loud why they had not seen the Conductor for nearly fifteen hours.

Joseph Miller, the Steward, was standing nearby and he leaned over to hiss at them, "The man is sick and taking a day off. Leave it be!"

Once Miller left them Jupe continued to his friends. "If the Conductor is ill, he's likely to be in the back car. I spoke with him last night and he said he's been told about the mystery man in black by some other passengers. He also said he's not the one scheduled to make this run but had to fill in. I have to say he sounded suspicious and more open to when I told him that before. Maybe if we could get back there and into that car, we could probe him for more information and perhaps even see if he'll lend us the keys to go to the front car. Something really strange is going on and I think it has to do with some members of the crew."

After dinner they headed to the observation car and then waited until most of the people on the downstairs area had gone to have their meals.

The connecting door at the back was behind a partition of fancy glass with gold-painted scrolls and patterns.

Jupe stepped around the edge just as the door slid open and the Chief Engineer stepped into the car.

"And, just what do you three think you're up to?" he asked blocking the corridor with his wide shoulders in case they tried to escape. He wasn't angry, just sounding tired.

"We are," Jupe told him matter-of-factly as he turned to face the man, "trying to find out why the Conductor goes into this car at least five times a day in the last three days, and why he comes out looking like he doesn't want to be caught. We've already caught him smoking in the corridors at night. Oh, and here..." and he handed the large man one of their cards.

"Seen that, son," the man explained but pocketed it rather than handing it back. "Now, tell me why you think our Mr Donlevy might be doing something he shouldn't. Other than the smoking inside that is." He looked as if nothing short of a full explanation might suffice, so the boys started telling him about everything that had happened.

Jupe began with their understanding from one of the Stewards that the Conductor had taken ill and was probably in the sleeping car.

"The only thing that is a real puzzle to us," he explained to the older man, "is that I keep running into Mr Donlevy outside the door of the third compartment in the car in front of ours. He is just standing there and has practically taken my head off, twice, over being in the corridors at night. Except last night he sort of confided in me he's heard about the mystery man I'd been chasing from some other people on the train. Adults!"

The Engineer suggested they all sit down.

After fifteen minutes Jupe tried to summarize. "Every time one of us spots the man in the mask and cape and try to chase him, your Conductor seems to be right in the way as we enter the car in front of ours. He stops us and never, ever seems to have heard or seen anything. It is strange and too much to be a coincidence that he has stopped one or all of us five times so far this trip. Then he goes and disappears for hours. As of now," and Jupe looked at his watch, "nobody has seen him all day. The last time anyone heard anything it was one of the Stewards and he said Donlevy had headed to the back of the train. It's just too bad only he has the key to this car."

The Engineer shook his head. "Not true. I told you only he had the keys to the side compartment in the first car behind the forward locomotive. I have the passageway keys for up there and back here. How the heck do you think I can get into either locomotive or give you guys that tour? Climb outside and run up and down the roof?" He let out a laugh that sounded more like a seal bark.

Still chuckling he stood and moved past the boys, around the partition and unlocked the doors. As he slid the back car door open an unpleasant odor wafted into the car where the boys stood.

"Oh-oh," Jupe said under his breath. He recognized the smell. "Uh, sir? Didn't you just come through that car? Didn't you smell that?"

The Engineer shook his head. "When the rear locomotive is running like it is now, and I spend ten or more minutes in there, as I did, the diesel fumes kills my sense of smell for a good twenty minutes. I could put a hunk of limburger in my nose and wouldn't smell a thing!"

He took a sniff and shrugged. "I'm getting a little something," he told them. "Somebody must have left some food out," the man said as he knocked on the firstly door in the passageway. There was no answer and he knocked louder. Again, no answer so he slammed his fist against the door and bellowed, "Open the door, Donlevy! That's an order!"

"I don't think he's going to answer," Jupe said. "I think that smell is what you get when you leave a dead body out in a warm space." He felt like throwing up and turned away.

The man tried his keys and they refused to turn the lock. Reaching for his small radio the Engineer made a call for the train's mechanic.

"Aft car compartment locked and lock is jammed. I need access pronto!"

When the man arrived less than two minutes later he was a little out of breath.

"Ran... all... the... way..." and he wheezed once, "... You... want... that... door opened?" he asked between deep breaths. "Something stinks to high heaven!""Yep! Get that open!"

It was the work of but a minute to punch the lock out and he had the door handle turning using a small pack of fine tools he carried in one of his many pockets.

Stepping back he allowed the Engineer to open the door When it was open, they all wretched at the stench of death that rolled over them.

Jupiter opened one of the side windows to get some fresh air in the corridor and then took a deep breath before taking a close look inside.

Sitting on the floor, his back up against a packing case that stood open was the Conductor. A large kitchen knife stuck from his chest just about where his heart was.

He must have died immediately, the First Investigator thought before he had to retreat and get a new lungful of fresh air. And, just when I was about to accuse him of being the man in the cape and the one behind all this.

Drat!

17

The Journey Must Continue

IT WAS a busy day inside the train with it now stopped in a small town called Lake Charles. The Engineer decided to continue to Lake Charles because it not only had a small station, it had a nearby airport. They had arrived about 4:09 AM and no announcement had been made until breakfast service began at 6:30. It had been greeted with groans and complaints.

Now, about 8:40, there were police officers combing the entire train looking for clues into the death of Mr Donlevy, the Conductor. Everyone who had spoken to the man had to go through an interview, alone, so the boys had to each answer the same questions.

√ When did you last speak with him?

√ What were you doing up that late?

√ What exactly did he say?

√ Why did he say he was waiting in the corridor?

√ What was he wearing?

√ Did he seem worried about anything?

And many, many others.

And then, because this train crossed state lines, four agents with the FBI evidently flew in from their Dallas office getting to the train just before noon, and the questioning began all over again.

When it was his turn an hour later, Jupe was ushered to the front of the dining car. There was one other table with a passenger and FBI agent at the other end and nobody else other that the man at his table.

"My name is Jupiter Jones and I live in Rocky Beach, California," he dutifully told the agent sitting across the dining table from him after hearing the first, and obvious, question. As he said this he reached into his back pocket and took out his wallet. From this he took the three special pieces of paper he hoped would make some difference to the man who appeared more bored than eager to find the bad guy.

"If you would, please, sir, take a look at these?" He handed the business card to the agent and set the other two pieces face up between them.

The agent looked at the card and was about to gently toss it back when his eyes caught the FBI seal on the most recent note. This he picked up and read carefully, twice, before standing up.

"You stay there. I'll be back." With that, he walked back to the observation car.

He came back five minutes later, his attitude changed. As he sat down he handed Jupe's FBI note back.

"Agent Anderson is held in very high regard within the agency, son. I had to go call to verify that you didn't just type that up. It's real and he tells me you and your two friends are the real thing as well, and you helped him solve a really important case a couple months ago. And, he says to tell you hello." Now his brow crinkled in thought. "How do three teenage boys become such great investigators?" he asked earnestly.

Jupe told him the whole story about how they had first solved a missing cat mystery and then a few other minor things the local police would have nothing to do with, but were important to the people they had happened to.

"Then, Mr Alfred Hitchcock—you know, the famous movie director?—well he heard about us and started asking us to come to the studio and report our cases to him, and he had some different writers turn those stories into, well, stories for him to read. He did that until he died a while back. We've been really successful and if you will listen to what I have to tell, we have a deeper mystery than Mr Donlevy's murder going on on this train."

The agent, Steve Barber, nodded, and he and Jupe spent the next hour going over everything from the mystery man in black to the counterfeit money and marijuana to the sightings of the Steward in El Paso and San Antonio and the beating they took in the first city and... so much more.

To his credit, the agent wrote down nearly half a small notebook of notes. Finally, he closed it, pushed his pen into his shirt pocket and folded his hands in front of him.

"Okay. Now let me tell you that we've had a suspicion about this train and its runs back and forth, but never had any proof. We've even had agents posing as passengers and they found nothing. Saw nothing and heard nothing as well. Frankly, we've been stymied until this death."

Jupe was thinking that if the agents they had assigned for that work looked anything like Agent Barber, anybody with eyes could have spotted them in about half a minute. He did not say that aloud, however...

"Murder," Jupe corrected him suddenly wishing he had not said that.

"Quite. I believe you saw all the clues we did and they certainly spell out murder."

Agent Barber suggested the boys keep the money where they has secreted it, but only after he had Jupe take him to the spot and show him where it was.

Barber took a look at Jupe's small camera and praised the youth on his ingenuity and asked if he might be able to rig it up to take pictures of anyone trying to open the air vent.

"Sure. I've got pretty much what I need except for some more super thin thread for the camera trip system."

Barber assured him he would have a spool of it before the agents left the train. He then spoke into a hidden microphone in his jacket lapel describing what the youth needed and then listened. "Good. Out!" Turning to Jupe he smiled. "You'll have it in twenty minutes. Uh, one thing more. Will we get anything else from your two partners?"

That simple question made Jupiter Jones feel more important than anything else. To be asked if his words told the complete story and to have this agent acknowledge that the three boys were legitimate partners made his heart sing.

"No, sir. I'm pretty much certain I've told you everything except for how scared Bob and Pete said they were when they confronted the man in black."

The agent shook Jupe's hand and thanked him.

"Listen, Jupiter. Two things. I recognize who you once were back on TV, and back then you impressed me as being the smartest one of the entire bunch of kids, and *honestly* smart, not script smart. The second thing is, when you get out of college, come apply with the FBI; I'll lay you a bet you will pass the tests and be asked to join us. Likely the same for your friends if that is what they would like to do. Oh, and thank you!"

Bob and Pete found Jupe standing in front of the windows outside their compartment an hour later. Like most of the passengers, when not being questioned they had been herded into the station and kept in the large baggage room.

"What's been going on?" Pete inquired seeing the smug look on Jupe's face.

"Yeah," Bob said, "and why did they tell us we don't need to be questioned?"

They entered the compartment, closed the door and sat on the sofa that could fold out to be Jupe's bed. There, he told them about his conversation with Agent Barber, the praise the federal agent heaped on the three of them, and how two other agents assisted him in setting up his camera device to capture anybody who even got close enough to look into the vent for the fake money.

"We created a sort of spider web of a very fine and nearly invisible filament that can flex but if it does by more than a half-inch it starts the camera. They will have an agent, possibly even Agent Barber, waiting for us when we get to New Orleans, and," now he was sounding very excited, "he told the Chief Engineer that if we need to call for assistance or to report anything we are to be given priority access to the train's radio telephone!"

The boys told Jupe they could all go off the train if they had been questioned but had to remain on the station grounds.

"I'm ready to stretch my legs," the portly boy announced, so they left the compartment, carefully closing the door and placing another hair across the gap before walking to the door and stepping down to the platform.

Another agent checked his list and nodded, "Yes. You three are cleared for..." now he took another, closer look. "Agent Barber says you are cleared to move wherever you wish, even off the station premises. Gee. Lucky you three!"

They walked down the platform and into the station and took a look around. Quite a few of the passengers were standing or sitting around, all looking bored and a little put out by this additional delay. As they passed one small group —including the same woman who had tried to tell them they needed her to watch out for them—who was saying, "I just don't understand this. They say someone has been killed but I haven't seen anybody who has been killed. Have any of you?"

Her husband, looking like he wanted to sink into his seat and disappear finally had had enough. "Penelope! Shut the heck up! If someone has been killed on this train, can't you make that tiny brain of yours think of anything other than your discomfort or how your narrow field of vision has not been affected? For criminy sake, just sit down and stop talking. Nobody wants to hear you!"

The husband sat down but as Jupe and Bob and Pete passed, they turned their heads in time to catch her plopping down on the bench with a sour look on her face.

"I guess what my dad said is true," Bob stated. "People who can't vacation together ought to never get married!"

Pete was about to comment on the fact the woman might have a better time or at least be a better companion if she took the look of superiority off her face. But, at that point the boys reached the outside doors of the station and looked out at the trees around them. The Lake Charles Station was in a desolate part of the town with what looked, and smelled like a sewage treatment plant across the tracks and to the left a little, and there were many trees and a couple buildings between the front of the station and the nearby freeway.

But, not much else.

Except, coming along what Pete found out later was Ryan Street, and sticking close to the trees so he could remain in shadows, was their old pal and suspect, Steward Miller.

He must have spotted them because he ducked behind a clump of trees, peeked out from behind one at least five times, and stayed there until the boys decided to move to the east and across a road.

"Let's sort of glance back to see if he make a break for it across the parking lot," Pete suggested.

The took turns and before they had walked more than fifty feet down what was signed as South Railroad Avenue, Miller had pulled the black hat he was wearing down to cover his face and had run to the west end of the station, disappearing around that corner

"That's not suspicious at all," Jupe said sarcastically as they turned around and headed back to the station.

"I hope one of the agents caught him sneaking back," Bob asserted.

"If not, I'll go tell Agent Barber. I'm sure he'll want to know that the Steward had left the train and gone for a walk. To somewhere—"

18

A Glimpse of the Ghosts for Everyone!

THEY FINALLY got underway at nine that evening. Dinner, of course, was late but people were so tired they didn't have the energy to complain and finished eating quickly before heading to bed.

Tomorrow, everyone hoped, would be a new and better day!

Bob has tried to convince the train representative who had also flown in, from New Orleans, that he ought to be given a ticket from the Lake Charles airport to Houston and then back to L.A. so he could get home in time to save his job.

"Sorry, kid. Once that voucher of yours was stamped, we're responsible for you and those other kids who won the contest and can't make an exception. You understand; we're just looking out for your welfare."

"Not really. Your way of doing things will get me fired by the time I finally get back."

The woman had just shrugged and walked away from him.

When he told the other two, Jupe stated, "Well, then maybe you'll have time to pay more attention to that girl in Geography class who keeps smiling at you. What's her name? Carly?"

"Kelly," Bob corrected him absently without looking up to see that Jupe was smiling at him, trying to drag him back from the brink of being depressed.

Just as the boys were getting ready to stand up and go to their compartment, the Chief Engineer walked up to them.

"Thought I'd find you here since I knocked on your door and there was no answer." He sat down on a chair across the meandering aisle down the middle of the car. "Listen. I have a favor to ask. Now," and he lowered his voice, "we all know about the tricks that give us the ghosts on this train and..." he paused as a man and woman came into the car but turned around and headed back into the dining car a moment later.

"Anyway, you three know how we do them. We need to give the folks a show to take their minds off all this nastiness and the delays and such, so we're putting on a ghost extravaganza tonight. In about an hour. Shrieking and flying all over the place and disappearing all of a sudden. What I need you three to do is *not* blow the trick. Stay here or in your compartment but don't come out and tell people there's nothing to worry about."

The boys agreed but Jupe asked for a favor in return.

"If possible I'd like to watch the action from the control car up front."

"Well," the man thought it over a moment, "it's all pretty much on automatic once the... oh, it is supposed to be the Conductor. Hmm. Okay, tell you what. If I show you what to do, will you only do that and then just sit back keeping an eye on things. And, hit the override button if anyone comes out and grabs onto one of our ghost friends? It'll drop and that generally has the passengers spooked enough to let it go and run away!"

Jupiter readily agreed and the Engineer took them to the front of the train and into the control room and showed them everything they needed to do.

"You can switch the main monitor there to each of the cameras in the front and back of each car," and he indicated the keypad with each camera's button.

"Can we see the dining and observation cars as well?"

"Sure those four buttons down the side and from the back-most observation car camera to the front one in the dining car." He pressed them and showed the trio what sort of views they could expect.

Jupe said nothing but was secretly pleased to see the back dining car camera could see right into the small side kitchen.

Before he went forward to tend to his night driving duties, the Engineer made certain all their watches were set to the same time.

"Remember, sometime between ten and ten-fifteen start the show. Not right on the hour or quarter hour, though." He turned to leave but turned back.

"If anything goes funny or you have troubles, one of you come forward to the engine. The door won't be locked but you need to not touch anything as you come to the front. Once you get there, knock on the door and stand back. By law I have to look through a peep hole and verify you aren't hijackers." He grinned. "As if someone would hijack this old girl? Ha!"

He left them and the boys spent the next fifty minutes checking each of the cameras to see what they showed. Only one had anything interesting and that was just a man and his —they assumed—wife necking at the very front of sleeping car four.

"Try another view," Pete requested.

Jupe pressed the button for the back of the dining car. He immediately leaned forward on spotting the suspect Steward, Miller, standing inside the kitchen pulling on a cape over his black shirt. It was a black cape! And, hanging on a pot rack to his side was a wide-brimmed black hat.

At least he and the other two assumed it was all black. The cameras for the kitchen were black and white and not color so if pressed they would not be able to attest to the exact colors, but the more he put things on and wrapped the cape around his shoulders, the more they were certain he was the mystery man in black!

Looking around them it was Bob who spotted the video recorder in a rack to their left. He walked over, found a fresh cassette in its wrapper and soon had it inserted.

"See if we can get any of this on tape," he suggested.

Jupe knew what button to press as it as marked **VHS DECK**. Now, he believed—or at least hoped—whatever they had on the main monitor would be fed into the recorder.

They watched as Miller in his disguise reached around the partition separating the kitchen from the small hall into the dining car and flicked a switch plunging the car into partial darkness.

Fortunately, they now found that the cameras worked very well in low-light conditions.

From car to car, back camera to front camera, they followed Miller as he made his way forward.

"Hey Jupe," Pete said. "I've got an idea."

He leaned in and whispered into the lead investigator's ear making Jupe smile and nod.

Seconds later, the plan was put into action.

As Miller approached the third car forward, coincidentally their car, the computers began the "Ghost Show" and the sounds of moaning and distant voices complaining about "no longer in our home!" could be heard.

Miller looked up, startled by the noises for a moment, but then he continued forward. A second later one of the "ghosts" came out of its hidden compartment at the front of the car and headed for the man. It brushed right into his face causing the man to let out a gasp and as they watched, Miller began swatting at imaginary ghosts.

When he wasn't battling the ghosts he was pushing past

passengers coming out to see what the noise and thumping was about.

Jupe took hold of the override joystick and began sweeping the ghost forward and backward over and into Miller.

By this time the noises had several passengers out of their compartments all watching this show.

A woman at the back of the car screamed and as Jupe switched cameras they could see her husband dragging her back into their compartment.

Switching back to the other camera they were in time to watch Miller get himself free and dash to the front door and into the next car.

Jupe was waiting for him with that car's ghost sitting right in his way. He tried to brush past it but as he stepped forward, Jupe moved the ghost forward just keeping it out of arm's reach.

Miller let out an angry roar waking up just about everyone in the car and causing several doors to open.

"What in the name of the seven devils of Rome is going on?" one man demanded. He appeared to be brandishing a rolled up magazine which he took to beating Joseph Miller on the head with.

Miller bellowed at him and raced for the next car.

Jupe and his friends had a lot of fun repeating variations of the ghost attack until two cars from the front where Miller pulled out some keys and opened the side door.

Seconds later he had disappeared out and up to the top of the train.

Jupe switched to the next car and then the car to the back. When Miller did not reappear he continued moving to each remaining car until they got back to the dining car.

Five minutes later, and looking wild-eyed, Miller suddenly appeared in the kitchen and ran to the back, through the observation car and into the sleeping car.

"Good, Let's hope our Mr Miller has learned a lesson that it isn't nice to tangle with this train's official ghosts!" Jupe declared.

Over the next fifteen minutes they reviewed the tape and all three Investigators were happy with the results. In at least five places when his hat either fell off or the brim flipped up, it was possible to plainly make out the face of Joseph Miller.

19
Every Clue Combines Into the Solution

IT WAS just five minutes before the train pulled into New Orleans when the boys left their compartment with their packed bags. They headed to the back hoping there might be some fruit of other snacks set out in the dining car.

"Good morning, Agent Barber," Jupe called out to the man's back. He'd just entered the train and was heading for the dining car.

Turning quickly, Barber smiled on seeing the three boys coming along the passageway. "Well, well. I'm glad to see that you all survived the last few hours. Do you have anything to report to me? And, is our little package all safe and sound?"

Jupe pulled the wrapped bundle of counterfeit bills from a satchel he'd borrowed from Pete and handed it over to the FBI agent.

"I believe you will find some very telling fingerprints inside that outer layer," he mentioned pointing at what looked to be four or five very clear, oily prints. "The open end is the only place my fingerprints will be found and I've taken the opportunity to produce a card with my prints for you to have. It's in the envelope in the bag."

"Jupe! That's my bag!" Pete reminded him.

"You boys wait here and I'll get this transferred into an evidence bag and bring this back. Give me five minutes. It's going to get a little exciting around here."

A minute later they heard Agent Barber's voice over the Public Address system.

"Ladies and gentlemen, and also our teenage guests. This train is closed off. Nobody will be allowed on or off until the FBI is finished with our investigation, the one you were all part of in Lake Charles. Please be patient and remain exactly where you are at the moment. If that is your compartment, do not step out. If you are in the observation or dining cars, remain seated until we get to you.

"It is a Federal offense to disobey these orders. Anyone attempting to get off the train for any reason will be subject to immediate arrest, seizure of anything you might be carrying off the train, and will be transported to a jail cell. The Bureau thanks you all for you cooperation, even though we realize this is a major inconvenience to you."

The boys took a seat at their table and watched out the windows as more than twenty agents and police officers surrounded the train, sealing it off.

They also watched as the woman they had dealings with before and her husband tried, unsuccessfully, to get off the train and into the station. Within seconds both were handcuffed, and the woman promptly fainted.

"Probably browbeat that poor man and now she has, what the movies and old books called, 'swooned' or come down with 'the vapors' or something silly women do," Jupe told his friends.

Twenty minutes later Agent Barber came back and took a seat.

"Well, your suspicions about there having been a dead body in that room were correct. We sprayed a special mist over the storage area and it glowed under some special lights telling us there was blood in there recently and also a sniffer dog they brought it went right to that room's door and sat down, her indication of a cadaver.

As they were talking, Bob spotted movement in the kitchen.

He tapped the agent on his hand and pointed to that area. Barber pretended to yawn, saying, "Boy, I sure hate getting up this early in the morning just to come down to New Orleans to search a train." As he was saying this he peered around and caught site of someone in there trying to move to a ladder set in the side of the train.

Barber picked up his lapel and softly said two words. "Ramjac" and "Food."

"Well," he told The Three Investigators, "I have to go back to the front of this thing to help search for more suspects. You boys stay here and I'll be back in, oh, thirty minutes."

He walked to the front of the car but stopped outside the kitchen, drawing his service gun, a rather nasty-looking .45 calibre pistol. He stood straight and silently with his back against the partition and waited.

The boys saw this and immediately decided, without even discussing it, to turn away and go back to watching outside.

Whoever it was—and Jupe would bet dollars to doughnuts it was the Steward, Joseph Miller—in the kitchen wasn't completely quiet as he climbed the ladder, threw a hatch in the ceiling open and climbed out of the car.

"He's out," Jupe announced loudly enough for their FBI man to hear.

This time as he spoke into his lapel, he was heading around the partition and to the ladder. "Suspect has left the dining car via to top of the train. All outside agents and police on my frequency, eyes up. I do not know if suspect is armed, but if he appears to be, shoot to disable, not kill. Repeat, do not shoot to kill unless he begins shooting at people."

Those words, more than anything else, made this feel as if the boys had been in danger. If the FBI was talking about killing the man, he must be a very bad one.

Barber's legs disappeared up to top of the ladder and they could hear him running toward the front of the train shouting at his adversary.

"STOP. Get down on the train and drop——" The rest was lost at both hunter and hunter got too far away from the open hatch.

Seconds later there was the sound of a gun going off. It made the boys jump in their seats. The sharp cracks rang out twice more and then ceased.

Jupe looked at his companions. They looked back at him and at each other. Nobody said a word but they all were saying silent prayers for Agent Barber and everyone else other than Joseph Miller.

"You young men want something?" came a soft female voice. It startled them as much as the gunshots, but they looked up to see the young woman chef of the train.

"Sorry if I scared you. I was hiding in the supply cabinet when Miller was trying to stay out of sight. The shots made me think he was gone so I came out. So, any food?"

They all said that cereal would be fine so she went to the kitchen to bring them some small boxes.

As she was working, Agent Barber came into the car, though the adjoining car, followed by three policemen and another plain-clothed agent. Between them the handcuffed and shackled Joseph Miller, and he was dirty as if he'd been dragged off the train top and was limping rather severely.

"Sit him down," Barber said and grabbed several cloth napkins. He folded one into a square and placed in over the bloodiest part of the criminal's pant leg, then used two more to tightly tie around the leg.

"That'll get him to the hospital," he said to the officers. Picking up something he'd dropped while he worked on the wound, he opened it. "Well, well, well," as he pulled black clothing, a black cape and hat from the athletic bag. "Looks like our Steward was also the man scaring people on the train. And my bet is we'll find his prints on that bundle of phony bills."

"Don't forget the bundles of what looked like marijuana we saw in the dead man's room," Jupe reminded the agent.

Miller's mouth dropped open. He looked like a man who had believed he was going to get away with something only to have the rug of truth yanked from under him.

The agents pulled Miller to his feet.

"You ruined this. Now I'm gonna have to go to jail and all because I don't want to get killed for snitching!"

As he is being hauled off, the lead agent turned to Jupe, "I guess Agent Anderson had you three pegged. Great investigation and pretty much wrapped up and handed to me. For that, I thank you."

"You will want to get the Engineer to let you into the front car—the one just behind the locomotive. In there is a recorder with a VHS tape you will need to see and take to court. We managed to get Mr Miller all dressed up in his mystery man clothes and heading to the compartment where the counterfeit bills had been stored. He was really tearing the place apart, so you'll likely get some good prints from in there as well!"

Barber stopped and smiled. "Do any of you have an idea what Miller was doing when he left the train in El Paso, San Antonio and Houston?"

Jupe nodded. "I'm afraid that the counterfeit bills may not have been the only one when the train left L.A. I think Miller was delivering smaller bundles of drugs along the way."

Barber nodded. "That's just what the Bureau believes. Good working with you three!"

* ? ? ? *

Jupe, Bob and Pete looked around at the station in New Orleans. Not as impressive as the starting terminal—it was rather gray and boxy—it marked the end of their Ghost Train adventure.

"I'm not going to be sad leaving that behind. Remind me to not enter any more radio contests," Jupe told his companions as Bob hailed a taxi to get them to the airport for their return flight home. Before it pulled to the curb the police car taking away a very angry former-Steward, Joseph Miller, who would be facing so many charges it was likely he would never taste freedom, left the station.

As the three boys stepped into the boarding area of the terminal at Los Angeles International, they were met by Jupiter's Uncle Titus who was, for some unfathomable reason, dressed up in his finest Sunday suit.

He even had his large and black moustache waxed and curled up at the ends, something Jupe had only seen when he'd gone to a funeral.

He hugged all three of them saying how happy he was they were safely back in Southern California.

"I've never seen you dressed up, Mr Jones," Pete told him as they walked toward the escalator to go down to Baggage Claim. "Surely you didn't have to get fancied up for us!"

Jupe could see the smile playing around his uncle's lips but said nothing.

"Just thought since this was a special occasion... well, you know. You boys being the big travelers now."

Once bags had been retrieved he led them toward one of the exit doors. Outside, pulled up next to the curb, was a Roll-Royce automobile the boys immediately recognized. And standing next to it in his very best chauffeur livery stood Worthington, their on-call chauffeur and friend for many years. He reached over and opened the rear door bowing to them as they trooped inside and took seats.

In a flash he had the door closed and ran around to get into the front driver's side.

"The arranged location, Mr Jones?" he inquired.

"Absolutely, Mr Worthington. And, as I explained you are to join us once you get this beast parked."

"Very good, sir. If you are certain…"

"Wouldn't have it any other way!"

The boys remained quiet for nearly ten minutes as the Rolls wound its way out of the serpentine roads surrounding the main L.A. airport. Then it raced along several streets until it finally turned into the parking lot of what appeared to be a very fancy restaurant.

"What are we doing here?" Jupe asked. "I thought we were heading back to Rocky Beach and home."

"Not quite yet," Uncle Titus told him. "Okay, boys. As soon as Mr Worthington has the door open I want you to follow me inside. No jumping out and running ahead, understood?"

The boys told him they would behave.

When he got the front door open a pretty young woman in an evening dress met them with a big smile. "Your party is waiting for you, sirs. Please let me take you four back to them."

"We are waiting for one more who will be right behind us and— oh, there he is now."

The boys turned around to find that Worthington had shed his chauffeur's jacket and hat in favor of a dark gray suit jacket.

The woman took them through a maze of tables and into a private room at the rear of the main dining room.

Sitting there, and all in very nice clothes, were Aunt Mathilda, Mr and Mrs Crenshaw and Mr and Mrs Andrews. All stood as the boys entered and began giving them a round of applause.

Jupe, as usual, was the first to find his voice.

"What in the word is this all about?" He wanted to add, "and how can you afford this place?" but his uncle beat him to it.

"The Train company contacted us with its thanks for something they say you three did. Something about a ghost?" He raised an eyebrow. "An unscheduled Ghost?"

"Well, yes, but—"

"But nothing, young man," Aunt Mathilda broke in. "This is their way of rewarding you for what you did and for how well they say you handled your duties as detectives. And," she said, her eyes misting up, "I want to apologize to you three for never realizing what good work you have been performing. I never considered that you were so... professional!"

Jupiter hugged his aunt before taking one of the empty seats at the table.

For her part she turned to Worthington and he began regaling her with tales of The Three Investigators.

It had been a great vacation and adventure, but now Jupiter was rather hungry and looking forward to seeing what the menu offered.

20

A Final Visit with Hector Sebastian

IT WAS a week later that the Three Investigators rode their bicycles out to the building that had once been a restaurant called Charlie's Place. Over the few years they had known the current owner, famous author, Hector Sebastian—and his Vietnamese houseman, Hoang Van Don—a steady stream of workers had been helping Sebastian convert the disused structure into a fabulous home with an impressive view.

Not that there had been construction going on all the time... no, it happened only when the author received money from one of his many books or contracts for movies made from them. Because of this haphazard scheduling, the work that might have otherwise taken three or four months had stretched out over more than twenty-five of them.

"I see he's finally had the outside scraped and painted," Bob said as he tilted his head toward the now steel gray house. Once it had been a faded white with many places where it was peeling off. The roof, too, had been replaced and now sported reddish-orange terra cotta slate tiles.

As they parked their bikes the front door opened and Don came out, smiling broadly at them.

"Mister Hector is waiting for your presence on the back deck," he told them sweeping his right arm low and back toward the open door. "If you will kindly follow me?"

"Hello, Don," Jupe greeted the Vietnamese man. "Things are looking pretty neat."

"They are neat and clean as whistle," the Asian man agreed. "Please, you come this way now. He is waiting for you all."

They crossed a large area that had once been the front half

of the dining room for the former restaurant. Now, it had been divided into a least two areas with one visible archway between the front—a formal living room from the look of the furniture—and into the less formal room fronted by floor-to-ceiling picture windows. As the three teens could see, this was only about three-quarters the width of the living room.

Pete pointed to the right. "What's through that door?" he inquired.

"Mister Hector wants pleasure of showing off house himself. Please, come outside."

Usually quite informal and helpful, Jupe wondered what might have brought on this change of attitude in the man. He also wondered—based on a distinct lack of any smells coming from the large kitchen to their left—why there seemed to be nothing cooking. With Don, there usually was.

The sliding doors to the deck were open and a comfortably-padded patio chair could be seen to the right. In it sat a large man with dark hair that had begun changing to speckled gray during the time the three boys had known Hector Sebastian.

Where they had begun their detective careers reporting to, and being subtly assisted by, the famous film director, Alfred Hitchcock, once that man had passed away, they'd found themselves meeting with, and greatly enjoying, Hector Sebastian.

At one time a private detective, an injury sustained in a plane crash had sidelined him, eventually forcing him to give up that business. He walked with a permanent limp and frequently needed to use an ornate, hand-carved cane to assist him.

While undergoing his recovery and some therapy to try to give him better use of his crushed leg, Sebastian had decided to chronicle a few of his wilder exploits. After nervously sharing them with a friend who happened to be a literary agent he discovered that the man enjoyed the stories so much he asked for an even dozen of them to be collected in a single book.

That book, "*The Crippled P.I.*" had sold more than a half-million copies and that led to his first novel. Not quite as successful as book number one, he set out to write, "just one more," and it became a huge hit and made the *New York Times* bestseller list for fiction. That led to it being purchased for a big-budget Hollywood movie and *that* led to his moving from the East Coast out to be close to Hollywood.

"Please don't get up," Jupe told him as Sebastian turned and began to reach for his cane.

Settling back into his seat, he responded, "Thank you, Jupe. Welcome to the newly completed Manse Sebastian. I'd have called it San Sebastian... but you know, someone beat me to that fine name. Come and have seats while Don fetches us all icy drinks. I believe his newest line features pineapple juice, coconut water and some sort of fruit pulp he will not divulge the source of to me. Good cold, though, if a little pink." He sipped the last of his current tall glass and handed it to the houseman.

The boys pulled up chairs and sat.

A minute passed with nobody saying anything.

"Well?" Sebastian finally said. "Aren't you going to tell me about this interesting journey you all took?"

Jupe rolled his eyes, Pete looked anywhere but at the adult, and Bob squirmed uncomfortably in his seat. He finally spoke.

"I lost the notes," he admitted looking quite miserable about it.

"What? Lost your notes? How unfortunate. I was so looking forward to reading about the adventure. Perhaps you can all tell me what happened. Good story telling is the same for a book as well as for face-to-face. So?"

Jupe cleared his throat. "We got everything down and agreed it was exactly what happened, and then..." He couldn't finish; his emotions choked him up.

"Then, my *mother* happened!" Bob stated.

"Mothers often do, but what actually happened?"

Bob first, with assistance from the others, told the brief tale of him finalizing things three days earlier, setting the fifty or so pages on the edge of his desk and going over to the junkyard and Headquarters.

"When I got home that night I didn't think about them and went to bed. The three of us met that next morning to do some checks of Jupe's latest equipment and print some film and by the time I got home—" a small tear cascaded down his cheek —"they were gone! My mother had been in to straighten up my room and saw that the pages had slid off onto the floor. She said they looked like a bunch of used scrap paper with chicken scratchings on them so I must have meant to toss them in the waste basket and missed. She did that, then emptied it in the big bin outside just before the rubbish collectors came and took it all away!"

He seemed utterly despondent.

Hector Sebastian reached over and patted Bob on the knee. "It'll work out, somehow. In fact, I have an idea. You say the three of you talked everything over and agreed to the series of events, correct?"

Three heads bobbed up and down.

"And I shall assume those same events are still clear in your memories, especially yours, Jupiter?"

Three more nodding heads told him the answer.

"Well then, we shall not only recreate those notes, we shall get them in such good and neat order that nobody will mistake them again. We can even create a special cover sheet for them and bind them in a folder to make them look like a real manuscript."

"How?" came the same question from the three boys.

Now, Hector Sebastian struggled to his feet taking up his cane just as Don returned with a tray full of tall glasses with some sort of opaque whitish-pink liquid surrounding ice cubes. Each glass features a tall straw and a small paper umbrella.

"We are going to the office, Don. Please bring those and also grab a couple more chairs so everybody can sit."

A minute later they all sat near the large, mahogany desk of the author on which sat a computer monitor and a keyboard.

Jupiter's face split in a wide grin while the other two looked confused. It had all become crystal clear to him a moment earlier.

"What?" Pete asked seeing the First Investigator's face. Then both he and Bob turned to look at their benefactor.

"I suspect that Jupiter has surmised correctly. Do you want to tell them, or shall I?"

Jupe made a "go ahead" gesture so the author cleared his throat and began.

"I have this marvellous computer and word processing software I use for my books and notes, so why not simply start a brand new file and recreate either your notes as you all recall them, or we can sit down and write the entire story just as if we plan to have it published!"

All three boys cheered at the thought of having one of their exploits properly documented.

"And, I dare say I might suggest you letting me submit it to my publisher for consideration. Even starting books in the juvenile line can earn the author, or authors in this case, as much as twenty or thirty thousand dollars plus royalties on sales."

It was immediately agreed and the four of them, with Don appearing frequently to refill glasses and then to bring snacks and finally dinner, sat around Hector Sebastian watching his fingers fly over the keyboard as the entire tale unfolded. He was such a fast typist that any mistakes—immediately underlined in red on the screen—were fixed almost before the others could register them in their brains.

The following day Jupe had to spend at the junkyard and Bob at the Library—where he had kept his part-time job—but Pete rode up and he and Hector managed to complete three more chapters before he had to beg off.

"Jupe is the one who knows about that next stuff."

And, that was fine. What would eventually become eighteen or even as many as twenty chapters was almost a third finished.

"I have to tell you, Pete, this is the fastest I've ever put together a story that is sure to be at least 36,000 words or so in length. We can certainly wait for the others and another day."

Pete rode back to Rocky Beach that late-afternoon very satisfied with what was taking place.

"I just wish we'd had Mr Sebastian and his Word Processor before when all our other adventures happened!" he said out loud and to nobody in particular as he pulled into his driveway.

<—> ? ? ? <—>

And that, dear reader is what leads us back to the beginning of this book, the book version of the reclaimed notes of the time The Three Investigators solved *The Mystery of The Ghost Train*.

The boys and I completed entering of their story into my computer two weeks later and just in time for them to enjoy the 4th of July.

I had secured them a publishing contract with a very nice advance payment based on just the first four chapters.

They tell me they may take the rest of the summer off to recover from their *vacation*.

As for me, I have been hired to turn one of my novels into a Broadway play and so I shall, at least for the next year, shut my beautiful home here along the coast of California up, and my faithful Don and I shall be moving to a less spacious apartment in New York City overlooking the center portion of Central Park.

But, we will be back!

I hope to have to opportunity to see some of you once the play opens, and I certainly hope to have to opportunity to work once again with The Three Investigators!

Hector Sebastian

Also By Author, Hector Sebastian:

For readers curious about the two locomotives mentioned in this book, here are a couple photographs for you.

Locomotive like the one at the front of the Ghost Train...

...and, the one at the back of the train.

Made in the USA
Columbia, SC
05 October 2024

43706948R00083